A GIRL
CALLED CRICKET

A GIRL
CALLED CRICKET

Colleen L. Reece

Thorndike Press • Chivers Press
Thorndike, Maine USA   Bath, England

This Large Print edition is published by Thorndike Press, USA and by Chivers Press, England.

Published in 2001 in the U. S. by arrangement with Colleen L. Reece.

Published in 2001 in the U.K. by arrangement with the author.

U.S. Hardcover 0-7862-3277-3 (Candlelight Series Edition)
U.K. Hardcover 0-7540-4517-X (Chivers Large Print)

"Bill and His Team," by Pearl Towne Reece, found on pages 177 through 183, used with permission.

The text of this Large Print edition is unabridged.
Other aspects of the book may vary from the original edition.

Set in 16 pt. Plantin.

Printed in the United States on permanent paper.

British Library Cataloguing in Publication Data available

Library of Congress Cataloging-in-Publication

Reece, Colleen L.
    A girl called Cricket / Colleen L. Reece.
        p. cm.
    ISBN 0-7862-3277-3 (lg. print : hc : alk. paper)
    1. Children of the rich — Fiction.   2. Loss (Psychology)
— Fiction.   3. Ranch life — Fiction.   4. Wyoming —
Fiction.   5. Large type books.   I. Title.
    PS3568.E3646 G57 2001
    813'.54—dc21   2001027100

In memory of Uncle Ed,
long, lanky, and lean

prologue

His blazing blue eyes stared into the faded gray ones facing him so steadily. Above a haggard face, his flaming gold hair was disheveled, the result of restless, anxious fingers. Endless moments later he turned away, his face contorted by eerie shadows. "I can't do it."

"You must." The other man's inexorable manner prevailed. "There's no way except this."

A log shattered into pieces, sending a shower of sparks into the blackened chimney of the rude mountain cabin. Any pity lurking in the older man's face dissipated behind his hooded eyes. "The plans are made. It is too late to stop them. Can't you see?" His voice echoed against the aged walls. *"There is no other way!"* His shoulders drooped, as if the burden of his plot had grown too heavy to carry.

"You love her, don't you?" The golden head shot up, the dead eyes catching fire at the sharp question.

"Yes, heaven help me!" Pride warred with shame and defiance. "Can't you see this will kill any chance — not that there ever was one," he admitted bitterly. "But this, I just can't stomach it."

Every trace of weakness fled from the old man's terrible face. "And I have said, *you will*. Do you think I'll let a weak stomach interfere when there's a human soul at stake?"

The watching man crouched like a cougar ready to spring, noting the high color in his tormentor's usually pale cheeks.

"You not only will carry through as planned, you will start tomorrow."

"Tomorrow!" Tensed muscles rippled under a suddenly too tight shirt. For a single heartbeat he considered bolting from the cabin.

"Everything is taken care of." The low voice droned on. "All you must do is . . ."

At last the voice stopped. Silence blanketed the room. The young man walked heavily to the fireplace and stared, unseeing, into its dying embers. Every trace of boyishness had gone. A man emerged, lips set, scornful eyes fixed on his companion. In a final protest he cried, "How can you trust me? How do you know I won't —" he choked.

A half-smile curled over the gray-eyed face. "Strangely enough, in spite of everything, I know you are an honorable man."

"God forgive you if you're wrong!" His hands clasped convulsively, his face worked into lines too old for his years.

A passionate voice roused him. "If I'm wrong, I have no right to be forgiven — ever."

With a last gasp the fire burned out, leaving the cabin as dreary as the plot hatched within its walls. Darkness enveloped the bleak stage setting for the drama to follow. . . .

1

Charity Endicott slid her engagement ring from her finger and weighed it in her hand. How heavy it was! The large diamond, iridescent as the soap bubbles in her waiting bath, was surrounded with small emeralds that shot sparks from their sullen depths.

It's like Cliff, she thought with sudden clarity. A little too large and lavish for good taste, even in these "roaring twenties."

Her heart rushed to her fiancé's defense. He might be flamboyant but he was the man she loved — the childhood image of a knight in shining armor come true — in a red airplane, instead of on a white horse, she mused to herself. Cliff Marshall's handsome face danced before her, sending a warm glow through her slim body. It lasted through her bath in the sunken tub of her private bathroom and followed her into the sunny yellow adjoining dressing room. With new eyes she surveyed her surroundings. The storybook theme that shimmered in her mind about Cliff carried into her measuring look.

"It isn't true what they say about people who have always had luxury and don't appreciate it," she told the rich cream-paneled walls. "I still think this is the most beautiful house on Long Island, or anywhere else." She seated herself at her lavishly appointed dressing table, picked up a gold-backed brush, and let it trail through her long, blue-black hair. Again and again she brushed until the usual satiny waves obediently lay against her yellow chiffon negligee.

"Won't Cliff be surprised once you're married to discover the perfectly tailored Charity Endicott secretly wears yellow and white and icy aqua negligees! A real change from the image everyone else sees." Her near-black eyes crinkled and she laughed delightedly.

A pinkish stain crept over the flawless white skin that never tanned regardless of hours on the tennis courts and golf links. *Married.* Her life linked with Cliff's — forever. Suddenly the pink fled and with it much of Charity's buoyant mood. What if Cliff didn't see marriage as lasting? So many of their ruling set changed partners on a regular basis.

"Then I'll have to be so alluring he won't

have any desire to look elsewhere," she flung at the looking-glass girl before turning away.

A half-hour later she descended the carved, spiral staircase from her second-story suite into the main hall. Her tailored snowy skirt, silk shirt, and sandals gleamed in the filtered light and the green scarf carelessly tied about her throat deliciously matched the emeralds in her ring. Again she was struck with the beauty of her home and a little prayer of gratefulness winged upward. Cliff had been glad to agree their place was in the Endicott mansion after marriage. Even now the entire west wing of the third floor was being completely redone for their life together — an enormous bedroom, dressing rooms for each, even a study for Cliff done in browns and tans with a sharp dash of red for an accent.

Remembering Gramps's relief, Charity's wide mouth spread into a wicked smile. "Gramps" certainly did not express the dignity of her grandfather, *the* Charles Endicott, financier and millionaire, at least to the watching world who fed on every move of the East Coast noblesse. Charity paused. Could there be a different, softer side of Gramps, the same way she kept some of herself private from others?

The idea startled her.

It's been far too long since we really just sat and talked, she thought, admiring the tapestried wall. *Not since I entered college.* Suddenly she wanted to see Gramps, to ask him, what? How to make the strange inner longings disappear, feelings that had nothing, and everything, to do with Cliff?

Charity impulsively detoured toward the magnificent library, envy of half the collectors in New York, but was stopped by the well-modulated doorbell. The next instant a tall, sandy-haired man swept into the hall, brushing aside Jarvis the butler. "Darling!" Pure delight shone in his hazel eyes.

Charity lifted her lips for his kiss and the urge to discover the source of restlessness within her fluttered and died. How could any girl ask for more than the devotion of this well-tanned giant? Of all the girls on Long Island, why had she been so fortunate to attract him? Many others had tried, she knew that — Donna, blond and clinging; Suzanne, red-haired and seductive. She mentally shook herself: Cliff had chosen her — and she rejoiced.

The same gladness radiated through her over lunch at a quiet restaurant. Even the crab soufflé seemed better than usual when love flavored every bite. When Cliff ordered his third cocktail, however, Charity's uneasiness resurfaced.

"I wish you wouldn't," Charity told him quietly, unwilling to have her happiness marred by even the slightest incident.

"Why not?" He raised an amused eyebrow. "I can handle it."

"I know — but weren't we flying?" Her level gaze noted the quick thrust of color in his face.

"Not *were*, are. It's a perfect day to hop off and circle the island." He glanced through the spotless window pane.

Charity's gaze followed his. It *was* a perfect day, this day after she'd finished her first three years of college. Indescribable blue skies soared above darkest green trees, roses clambered like children in search of the sun, and in the distance blue water seemed to merge seamlessly with the sky.

"Why don't you ever take a cocktail, Charity?" Cliff asked and leaned forward. "I've even seen you turn down champagne and it's about as mild as fruit punch."

Her muscles tensed. A long-ago memory nibbled at her but she thrust it back and said briefly, "I once saw a terrible accident. The young girl had been drinking."

"People who can't handle their liquor shouldn't be allowed to drink," Cliff said virtuously. He drained his glass, stood, and smiled the slow smile that unnerved her every time. "Let's go. I have something very special to ask you."

Charity could feel her heartbeat quicken. Was he going to push for an early wedding, the way he had the last time they were together? It had taken all her strength to laugh him off then. On a day like this, with her heart soaring, it would be impossible. No wonder so many girls become brides in June! Magic air and sunlight were potent allies of romance.

Forewarned didn't prove to be forearmed. Charity stumbled for words when Cliff asked, "Have you decided to go ahead and marry me now?" His knuckles showed white against the steering wheel of the low-slung automobile.

"Why is it suddenly so important?" she responded in amazement. "When we became engaged a few months ago we agreed to wait until I finished college next spring. It's not as if there's any hurry. I won't even be twenty-one until late September."

"If you really cared about me, you'd want to marry me now."

Charity's eyes opened wide at the harsh tone. She'd heard it a few times with others but never with her.

"After all," he added thoughtlessly, "it isn't as if you're crazy about that college course."

Charity was effectively silenced. Cliff only parroted what she'd told him. The estates and business management courses her grandfather had pushed at her left her cold. If only she could have taken . . .

Cliff expertly parked the automobile alongside the private air strip he shared with two friends. "Good, no one else here," he exulted, and reached for her. "My best weapon, Charity . . ."

She was in his arms, weakening, feeling surrounded with the affection she'd longed for since her parents died when she was small. Why not give in? Marry Cliff and live happily ever after? A warning bell sounded deep inside. Even her love couldn't silence it. Why had he changed his mind about waiting? There was a certain restlessness about him, a carefully suppressed excitement, an urgency that troubled her.

She pulled away. "Cliff," she knew her voice sounded terribly small. "I do love you and want to marry you. But I promised Gramps I wouldn't marry until I was at least twenty-one. He wants me to be sure."

"Sure!" Cliff jerked away, eyes blazing. He uttered a rough oath, the first she'd ever

16

heard him use. "Why is it any of his business?"

"He raised me. He wants me to be happy." It sounded inane even to her own ears. Charity tore her gaze from his stormy face and glanced out the open window. If only he would understand.

"Then too, I've never really done anything before that could please him, except be his granddaughter. He wanted me to take the course so I would know how to handle the Endicott fortune when it comes to me." She turned back to him in time to catch a dying gleam in his eyes strangely reminiscent of the dull stare she'd seen in the heart of the emeralds. "Why, what —"

"You may as well know, I'm in a bit of a j—" Cliff broke off, frowned, then his face cleared. "Forget it, Charity. Let's fly." He bounded around the car, stumbled a bit as he bowed low, and opened her door. "M'lady, your humble servant awaits."

Charity's keen look saw through the fooling. Cliff's face was flushed, the way it had been a few times before after a long evening and several drinks. She started to step out but changed her mind. "Let's not fly today, Cliff."

"Why not?" he challenged. "Think I can't handle the *Charity*?"

The red two-seater plane had been promptly renamed *Charity* after they met six months before; it had been the *Red Wonder* before. How thrilled she had been the first time he took her up in it, hands steady on the controls.

Those hands weren't steady now. They twitched on her door. "Coming?"

"No. You shouldn't either, Cliff. Please, don't fly," she begged. "I have a strange feeling. . ."

"Nothing strange about my feelings for you." He bent down and kissed her. She caught the sharp whiff of liquor on his breath and his kiss changed. Always before there had been tenderness, even in the most exquisite moments. Now the masterfulness became something else, demanding, hot, insensitive to Charity's response, intent on gratification rather than allowing her to give freely.

She pulled away. "Cliff, what's come over you?" She could feel his anger. Sudden suspicion filled her mind. "Were you drinking before you picked me up?" She'd thought he'd been heavy-handed with his cologne. Besides, his well-stocked bar contained a lot of vodka and it left no telltale odor.

"Charity is certainly a good name for you," he tightened his lips. "You're turning out to be a real Puritan."

She could feel color rising up the neck of her white shirt. "You're going too far, Cliff."

Too enraged to catch the warning in her quiet words, Cliff leaned over her again and laughed unpleasantly when she automatically slid across the leather seat to avoid his cloying breath and flushed face.

"Get in, Cliff. I'll drive home." Charity turned on the ignition and the motor sprang to life in response, quiet, luxurious, barely audible.

"Not me." He lounged indolently against the passenger side, then straightened. "I'm going flying."

Fear mingled with disgust engulfed Charity. She clutched the wheel and pleaded once more. "Please, Cliff, don't go up today. We'll go back to our patio and talk about setting a wedding date." She hated herself for the compromise but her fear had grown to a giant, nameless dread. Anything to keep him out of the plane.

Triumph showed in his hazel eyes and a smile spread across his face but he didn't give in. "We'll go after I come back. After *we* come back." Charity stared in disbelief when he opened the car door and reached across to her. Was he planning to drag her to the plane? Fury broke through her fear.

"What do you think you're doing?"

Cliff jerked back and mumbled, "Can't reach you. I'll come open the door like a gentleman." He slammed the passenger door and strode in front of the car.

He couldn't mean it — *he did!* She saw it in the firm step and set jawline. He intended to force her to fly with him. Charity opened her mouth to protest again but read in his eyes that nothing she could say would change him when he was in this mood. Should she scream for help? She quickly surveyed the field and nearby estates. Not a sign of anyone.

He had rounded the left fender now, nearer, nearer. "What's wrong with you?"

Charity flayed herself. "Go — now!"

Cliff was clear, one hand reaching for the door. With one fluid motion Charity shoved the car into gear and slammed her right foot onto the gas pedal. The automobile leaped forward. In her rearview mirror she saw Cliff stop, lurch forward, then cup his hands around his mouth. Even above the roar of the enraged motor his words were clear, "You'll pay for this!"

Charity snapped her attention back to the road running parallel with the landing field. When she was far enough away that he couldn't get to her, she braked and stopped.

Nausea rose in her. How could Cliff have allowed himself to drink until he lost control? She buried her face in her hands. Broken dreams floated around her like dandelion puffs in the sunlight. Would she ever be able to trust him again? If they were married and he continued to drink . . . what then? Chaos claimed her mind.

It wasn't until she heard the roar of a plane engine that she lifted her tear-streaked face. She looked back. Cliff was already in the pilot's seat.

"Oh, God, no!" It was not a curse, but a prayer. Her disgust became determination. *Cliff must not fly in his condition.* Again she frantically looked for help. The only living things in her vision were a lizard sunning itself on a rock and a chattering chipmunk nearby. It was up to her to stop Cliff.

Charity whipped the convertible around. Faster, faster, if she could get in front of the plane on the runway he'd have to stop. Racing against time, against the taxiing plane, against the heart-pounding panic threatening to overwhelm her efforts. Across the paved strip, she clung to the wheel. Her teeth set in her lower lip until she tasted blood. Now she was aware of the danger to herself. If she couldn't head him off, if he wasn't sure enough to avoid her, she could be killed. She could feel the blood drain from her face but her foot never moved from the gas pedal. She was almost where their paths would intersect. Gladness swept away all else. Cliff would be safe!

Her hopes died at birth. With more dexterity than she'd given him credit for in his condition, Cliff expertly changed direction, not enough to lessen his takeoff, but enough to foil her plan to stop him. Only inches separated them as the *Charity* gathered speed, wobbled a fraction of a moment, and then soared into the sky above the tall treetops at the end of the runway. "Too late, darling," floated back.

Defeated, Charity strained her eyes after the vanishing red dot. For better or worse, Cliff was in the air.

"For better or worse," she repeated the words, aware of fatigue. She couldn't remember ever having been so tired after races or tennis or swimming. God help Cliff Marshall — he was beyond anything she could do except wait.

Charity managed to turn the automobile, get back to the edge of the field, and park the car. She slowly got out and walked to the hangar. Her feeling of desolation increased. Yes, he'd taken off, but what would happen when he tried to land? If only he'd stay up until some of the anger mingled with liquor subsided! Should she call someone? She could imagine herself telling the fire department, "I had an argument with my fiancé and he went flying when he shouldn't have. Yes, he's been drinking, I think too much. No, I'm not certain . . ."

Cliff would be even more furious. It would be bound to hit the papers, anything to do with the Endicotts always did. Cliff had a thing about publicity. He'd even refused to let his picture be run for their engagement. "Just run yours, darling," he'd urged. "No one wants to see my ugly mug." When copies came, Charity had thought the wistful-eyed bride-to-be looked lonely in the column.

She impatiently brushed the thoughts aside. There were far more important things to think of than his aversion to publicity. A low drone alerted her. She whirled toward the runway. Maybe one of the other owners had been out and was coming in. Charity held her breath, waited, then a low sob escaped from her throat.

The growing speck was scarlet, and far too low.

She abandoned the automobile and ran toward the field waving wildly. The red plane dipped its wings in response, lifted, and roared over her in a crazy arc against the sunny sky.

Again Cliff approached the runway, this time too high. For the second time Charity stood her ground. He circled and headed back. Even from where she stood far below Charity could see his drawn-back lips. She knew he must finally realize his danger — and hers. Closer, closer — "Too low!" she screamed.

The plane touched down, gathered speed, touched again, and then rushed at her like a devouring monster. Terror froze her to the spot. She couldn't move and her life depended on it. Endless moments passed in the space of a heartbeat as tragedy etched the Long Island scene: a red plane, skipping down a runway; a white-clad figure in its path; a pilot who —

"Watch out, Charity!"

Cliff's final scream shocked the girl into movement. She came alive, ran toward safety, kept on running, vaguely aware of wind rushing past her from a wingtip that barely cleared her body. Her sandal caught in a rough spot and sent her sprawling. Dazed, she barely managed to turn her body. The *Charity* was down, but at far too great a speed. Rushing, rushing to destruction at the end of the runway.

Even in her numbed state, she could be there when Cliff crashed, as she knew he would! Before she reached the parked automobile she saw in slow motion the slamming of a little red plane into the stand of tree monarchs guarding the airstrip. A resounding crash was heard, then all was still.

"Planes explode and burn," Charity said aloud as the automobile lurched toward the site of the crash. "I have to get him out." She was out of the car before it came to a complete stop next to a crumpled heap of metal and broken glass.

"I have to get him out," she repeated, snatching open the door and reaching for the unconscious figure strapped in. Inexperienced as she was with anything to do with accidents, she knew he was seriously hurt but not dead. A tiny pulse in his throat quivered, then slowed.

Boom! The remains of the *Charity* burst into flames.

"Good, now help will come." Charity knelt by her fiancé's side, desperately wishing she knew what to do. Blood welled from a gash in Cliff's forehead. She snatched off her silk scarf and stuffed it against the cut, trying with one hand to see where else he was bleeding. She talked to herself, unconscious of it, but babbling.

"Steady, Charity, slip your hand in his jacket." It came out red and she shuddered. "Rip his shirt." When she did, it exposed tanned skin marred by the same life-sapping streams.

In the distance she could hear sirens squalling their way through the sunny afternoon. For a single instant Cliff's eyes opened. They focused on her. "Help me, Charity!"

"I don't know how."

Her words were lost in shouts, the sound of heavy feet running. "I'll take him, Miss."

Charity sagged and looked into a concerned steady face. "I — I didn't know what to do."

"We're trained. We'll do everything we can. Is he your husband?" Deft fingers had already replaced Charity's stained scarf with sterile padding.

"No, my fiancé." Charity shivered as cool air touched her bared arms. When another helper tossed her his warm jacket she gratefully put it on and clutched its generous folds around her. "Will he — ?" she couldn't go on.

"He's badly hurt. Booze and airplanes don't mix." Gentle hands lifted Cliff's broken body to a stretcher. "Do you want to come in the ambulance or follow in the car?" She caught his significant look and a wave of thankfulness crept over her when he ordered, "Kelly, drive her to the hospital. She's had about as much as she can stand."

Charity silently followed the man called Kelly to the automobile, slid in, and rested her churning head against the seat back. If only she could think, or feel! The creeping paralysis of what had happened robbed her of speech and will — and what lay ahead might be even worse. She clenched her hands until the nails bit into her palms, took deep breaths, and tried to prepare herself. Shame and regret over her own inability to do anything but stand helplessly by tore at her heart and gnawed into her very soul.

2

Charity Endicott never knew if it took five minutes or five hours to get to the hospital. Her mind raced ahead of her body, urging the car forward through the streets, past well-manicured lawns and lofty homes. If Kelly spoke to her, it didn't register. All that mattered was getting where Cliff was being taken.

Once she asked, "Are we almost there?" and caught her breath in relief when Kelly said, "Almost." A few blocks on he swung into the emergency entrance of the nearest hospital and said, "Go ahead and get out here. I'll park the automobile and bring you the keys."

"Thanks." The smile didn't quite reach her frozen lips but it was the best she could do. She stumbled from the car and into the large room, aware of curious eyes on her.

"Right this way, Miss Endicott." A white-clad nurse in a trim white gown led her to a small empty room, but not before a reporter's flash exploded in her face, followed by a puff of smoke.

"Vultures!" the nurse commented, sympathy written over her features. "I don't know how they can get here this fast."

Charity didn't either. "Is Cliff — Mr. Marshall —"

"He's still alive." The nurse forced Charity into a chair. "Drink this." She handed a cup of coffee to Charity, who obediently sipped it although she usually hated it.

"I called your grandfather but he wasn't there. I left a message."

"How does everyone know who I am?" Charity's brain had begun working once more.

The kindly nurse smiled. "The Endicotts, and those around them, are always news." Frank curiosity shone in her eyes. "There's no keeping something such as this out of sight."

"No," Charity agreed, but her mind added, *Cliff will hate this and blame me.* However, there was far more at stake than his annoyance or blame. If Cliff lived, it would be months before he was himself again. Why should the thought give her a feeling she'd been reprieved? Guilt consumed Charity. She should be thinking of nothing except if he were going to make it instead of how the accident affected herself!

After the nurse left to attend to others, Charity sank back against the typical drab waiting room chair. If only she could get out of her stained, crumpled skirt and borrowed jacket. They made her skin crawl. She stared at her hands, still blood stained. At least she could wash. She started to get up, wondering if it were worth the effort and was stopped by a choking sound from the doorway.

"Gramps!"

The tall spare man leaped forward, color returning to the gray face that matched his smoky gray eyes and hair. "Cricket!" He caught her in an unaccustomed hug. Something warm and wet splashed to her hand and she looked up in wonder.

"I thought — you said you were flying —" His ashen lips stopped moving.

The truth hit her with cannonlike force. "You thought *I* was in the crash too?" She buried her face in the well-cut tweed jacket, feeling its roughness and glad for the sense of security it gave. "Didn't you get the nurse's message?"

"Message?" The watching eyes were bright under shaggy gray eyebrows when he held her off and looked at her. "The only message I got was from one of the estates near the field that said the *Charity* had crashed." His voice trembled. "I came here immediately. Knew they'd bring you. I didn't even wait for Hunt to drive me."

"I'm sorry, Gramps. It was all my fault." Charity rubbed her hot eyes with a dirty hand.

"Nonsense! How could Cliff Marshall's crashing be *your* fault?"

She could hear the disbelief in his voice. "We quarreled — he wanted to get married right away. He'd been drinking. I refused to fly with him. Maybe if I'd gone up, too, I could have —"

"Could have been killed right along with the young fool!"

"Gramps!" Her eyes opened wide with horror. "He's not *dead!*"

"No, no," Gramps slid his hands to her shoulders and forced her to look directly into his eyes. "But no matter what happens, remember, it is not your fault in any way."

Charity felt herself reel. If he hadn't been holding her she'd have crashed to the floor. "I couldn't do anything. I —"

"That's enough, Cricket." He shook her gently. "I'm getting you home and into some decent clothes."

The sound of the pet name no one called

her now she had grown up unnerved Charity even more. "Shouldn't I stay here?"

"No. Cliff is in surgery. Several doctors are working on him. He may even be flown into New York City to a specialist. There's nothing you can do. You wouldn't be allowed to see him if you stayed." He led her down what seemed a mile-long corridor past numberless doorways, some open, some closed against curious visitors. Busy nurses wove in and out, smiling at the tired girl and her grandfather. To Charity's excited mind they seemed a kind of miracle band, carrying knowledge and healing in their spotless, capable hands. She looked at her own usually immaculate hands. What a contrast! They could capably hold reins or a racket, but had been helpless when needed most.

She stumbled and Gramps put one arm around her, half-supporting her to the car. "Just a little farther, Cricket." They reached the shining sedan and he helped her in, then slid behind the wheel.

"I'll get the upholstery dirty," Charity said and sighed. "I'm not fit to be seen." Pent-up emotion threatened and she bit back a sob. If she once started crying the dam inside would burst with the force of Niagara Falls. Maybe it would help to talk.

"Gramps —" she began at the beginning. Nothing was held back. Everything tumbled out. Several times she saw her grandfather's hands tighten on the wheel. When she got to where Cliff reached to drag her from the automobile he growled low in his throat but didn't interrupt.

"And then he left — and came back." Was that colorless voice her own? "I got him out of the plane just before it exploded and burned. But there was so much blood! I couldn't do anything except try and stop it. Cliff opened his eyes once." She swallowed hard and forced herself to continue over the gigantic obstruction in her throat. "He asked me to help him."

Gramps raged, "Idiot! He knows what drinking does to anyone's senses."

Charity wasn't quite finished. "I had to tell him I didn't know how to help him." Fresh agony welled up inside her. *I didn't know how.*"

"Try and forget it," Gramps advised and swung the car into the long, curving drive that led to the Endicott mansion. Even the ranks of spruce and fir and the groomed flower beds didn't calm Charity. Too tired to protest, she went up the weary stairs to her room. Five minutes later she was immersed in the great tub and a maid had taken her ruined skirt and the jacket that must be replaced away.

Gradually the cleansing bath unknotted her muscles. By the time she toweled off and changed to apricot satin pajamas even the accident had lost power to keep her awake. She fell into her canopied bed and slept.

Charity awoke to a dim room with drawn drapes that allowed only a single ray of sun to seep through. She stretched, wondering why she was in bed. Had she been sick?

The whole day rushed back to attack her. Her moment of peace fled before everything that had happened in the hours between morning and early evening.

"Cricket?" A light tap at her door brought her upright in bed.

"Come in, Gramps."

He was followed by a maid, tray in hand. The thought of food sickened her. "Please, I can't eat."

"It's just a thin broth and a piece of toast."

Her rolling stomach settled a bit. To please Gramps she tossed an apricot negligee over her pajamas and struggled to get the broth down. She couldn't manage the toast.

"Have you heard anything more?" she asked as soon as the maid disappeared with her half-eaten supper.

"Cliff's been taken to the best physicians in New York City. Things don't look good. He lost a tremendous amount of blood — and the alcohol in him didn't help."

Charity crumpled her fingers in her satin lap. Unspoken words trembled behind her set lips. Maybe if she'd been better able to stop that blood flow Cliff would have had a chance. In spite of the warmth of her cozy room, she shivered from a sudden chill at the thought.

Gramps didn't miss a thing. "Go back to bed," he ordered. "I'll send up a glass of milk."

She read his concern in the way he tucked her in and awkwardly kissed her forehead. They weren't a touching family and the caress showed how much he suffered for her. He stopped at the door and smiled. "Things will be better in the morning, little Cricket." The next instant he was gone.

Charity fought back tears unfamiliar to her but ever present this dreadful day. Gramps had given his standard comfort, the one he'd used since her early childhood. Would things really be better in the morning? Would Cliff pull through? He had magnificent strength from sports and that should serve him in this crisis. Much of her feeling about his actions eclipsed into memories of happy times together: riding the skies in the *Charity*; skimming the seas in his new sailboat; spending weekends aboard friends' yachts; hurdling obstacles with their favorite jumpers.

She dutifully drank the milk when it came — and realized a little later crafty Gramps must have dropped in a sleeping tablet or two. She turned, tucked her head into one smooth arm, and slept again.

She awoke shaking, haunted by unremembered dreams. There had been danger, only there was no airplane. She had been somewhere she didn't recognize. Black shadows from tall objects pursued her. Hot and cold by turn she slipped from bed. The room felt stuffy. Achy and restless, she noiselessly slid back the drapes and opened her window wide. Fresh night air rushed in and enfolded her. How still the garden was below! If she could get outside without being heard, she'd turn the water on the laughing girl statue Gramps said looked like her. It would be beautiful in the starlit night.

Like a pale ghost she stole downstairs. The great mansion was silent, the plush carpeting thick beneath her slippered feet. Even the lock on the carved front door was well oiled and made no protest when she slid back the bolt. With one foot on the wide porch she hesitated. The fresh air also felt cold. On impulse Charity turned to the huge hall closet and grabbed a warm coat that always hung there. Its hood would protect her from cold if necessary.

Step by cautious step she proceeded, across the porch, around the house, and off the terrace until she came to the garden just below her window. The fragrance of roses was everywhere and she sniffed greedily, filling her lungs with the sweet air. She had no trouble locating the faucet connection and watched the spray spring joyously up around the stone figure who forever laughed. A lopsided moon crept out from behind its protective cloud blanket and Charity drew in her breath at the unearthly shimmer of water drops.

A wrought-iron bench nearby, complete with cushions, looked inviting and she sank down into its depths, still facing the laughing girl.

She had been a laughing girl too. Friends made no effort to hide their envy of her lifestyle. Charity Endicott's heritage on Long Island had begun long before her birth and continued to the present with only a few disruptions. Her grandfather and his father and grandfather before him had ruled the spacious home and acres of land much like the feudal lords. They paid top wages to those who served them and expected perfection in return — and got it.

Only twice before had Charity faced such sadness. When her parents died she'd been so small she only remembered a beautiful lady in a white dress with a handsome father who used to set her in front of him on his horse. Her clearest memory of that time was Gramps saying, "Well, Cricket, it's just you and me now." She'd clung to him, not really understanding, wanting to make the sad look on his chiseled face go away.

As she grew, the name he'd given her at birth became just between them. To all others she was Charity, a name far more suitable for her position than Cricket. Once she'd asked him why he chose that name. She could still see the way his eyes had crinkled at the corners as he faced the indignant eight year old. She had just seen an enlarged picture of a cricket in her science book and demanded, "Why do you call me that? I'm no long-legged insect!"

"A cricket on the hearth sings and brings happiness to a home," Gramps said. Then, with a rare revelation, he added, "Your grandmother was my cricket on the hearth. Everywhere she went she brought joy to others, especially to me." As if ashamed of showing such mellowness, he glared at her from beneath his heavy eyebrows. "Now run along and don't get too big for your britches."

Charity's mouth curved in a smile. Gramps and his back-to-the-land expressions were the despair of Long Island society. So were his views on modern morality. Maybe that's why she had escaped falling in love until Cliff Marshall appeared. Oh, there had been beaux, Teddy Houston, Fred Colver, and Harrington Aldrich, to name a few. All sons of neighbors anxious to annex the Endicott estates to their own through a "suitable" marriage. They were good friends, men to dance and swim and ride with in races; they were escorts for social events and patrons of charity. Yet none had really touched her heart until Cliff.

With an effort Charity jerked her attention from memories of Cliff. A nagging thought, something knocking at the door of her brain and clamoring for admittance haunted her. She stared straight into the mystic, falling water and let herself drift. Ever since she'd knelt in the grass next to Cliff, and cried, "I don't know how to help," she'd subconsciously known she had to face the second harsh memory of the past, the knowledge of failure not once, but twice. . . .

★ ★ ★

"Gramps," Charity dashed into the library swinging a tennis racket. "I'm off for the club semifinals today." She made a mock slash at him with the racket. "Is there anything on earth more terrific than being seventeen years old, just graduated from high school, and looking forward to my debut?" Brief white skirts flew as she whirled and laughed into her grandfather's face.

He responded as usual. "Life's about what you make it." She could see the fondness in his eyes he took such pains to conceal so she wouldn't be "spoiled rotten," as he termed it.

"Come on, Gramps, don't you want to see me win?" she coaxed.

His manner changed abruptly. There was real regret in the face he turned to her. "I just can't. Something's come up and I made a doctor's appointment for a checkup."

"Gramps!" Charity dropped her racket, eyes enormous. "There isn't anything wrong with you, is there? I know you don't like going to doctors."

"Just a little tired lately." He smiled reassuringly. "He'll probably tell me to take vitamins or something, the old goat."

Her fear subsided. "He isn't any older than you are," she defended Dr. Carlson.

40

"He just acts older."

"His brain, except for medical knowledge, is fossilized," Gramps snorted and reared back in his swivel chair.

"There can't be much wrong with you or you wouldn't stay so ornery," Charity told him and blew a kiss over her shoulder when she got to the door. "Wish me luck."

"Do your best."

His words accompanied Charity to the garage. Hunt, their smiling chauffeur, already had her automobile polished and waiting. "Wouldn't you like me to drive you in the big car?" he asked hopefully.

"Of course not." She smiled the smile that made slaves of all the Endicott servants. "I'm still too proud of this little one Gramps finally let me get." She slid into the silver gray upholstered seat that matched the exterior and bounced with youthful exuberance. "I like this better than any of the big ones. Maybe because it's all mine."

"I thought you'd choose a fancy Cadillac," Hunt confessed. He removed an imaginary speck of dust from her right headlight.

Stubbornly she answered, "No. I like this one." She put the car into reverse and then circled and waved, her mind busy. She couldn't tell Hunt before she broke the un-

41

welcome news to Gramps that a showy automobile would set her too much apart at school.

A familiar rush of rebellion caused her hands to tighten on the wheel. She *wasn't* going to the prestigious finishing school of her grandfather's choice but to a nearby college where she could meet other than the rich and mighty. She wanted to know all kinds of people — good, bad, crusaders, even those who disagreed with her violently. She couldn't and didn't want to escape being Charles Endicott's granddaughter and sole heir; she simply longed for excitement and adventure. She had considered forgetting about having a debut. It seemed a little pretentious to her in the new modern America for certain pampered society darlings to be presented to the world. Wouldn't it be better to meet the world with something more to offer than social position?

When she casually hinted at such heresy, Gramps exploded. "Not that I care that much, either, but it was your parents' dream — so get out of your head any idea of skipping out." She'd seen he was in earnest so she drummed up a false enthusiasm. Gramps had been her world too long for her to cross him except for the important things, such as not attending finishing school.

Charity caught a glimpse of herself in the mirror. Just enough excitement at the thought of battle with her grandfather to send becoming flags of red flying in her white skin. Her red lips parted in a secret smile. "I can be stubborn, too," she told the passing countryside.

She glanced at her watch. Plenty of time to make it to the club and watch the other semifinalists. Or, her eyes sparkled, enough time to take the lesser traveled road, the one overlooking the sea. There would be little traffic in the middle of a workday. She swung the wheel and made a sharp turn, sniffing the salty air flowing through her open window. She let up on the gas, savoring every moment. Her busy high school years had left little time to be alone. Every spare moment free of study had been filled with sports, parties, and fun. She'd missed the long hours when she could read or walk or just think.

Charity sighed. This summer would be just as bad. Getting ready for her debut, preparing for college. Fortunately grades were no problem for her. She had stood at the head of her class since childhood days at the specially selected private school as easily as she had led whatever activity was happening.

A low hum turned to a dull roar then a deafening sound. Charity came out of her reverie and concentrated on the noise, coming closer now. Someone was hurtling down the narrow road toward her — had the brakes gone out? She hastily pulled as far to the right as she could, leaving most of the pavement for the oncoming car. It was a bad place, on the bend of a curve, with a narrow parking strip on the other side of the road giving way to a sloping cliff to the beach.

The next instant an older model sedan rounded the bend, far too fast. Charity caught a glimpse of terrified eyes and flying blond hair as the driver saw the parked car huddled against the fringe of the road. She frantically swung her wheel to avoid Charity and the sedan lurched. A final attempt to jerk it back to safety failed. With a horrid scream tires spun in loose sand. The sedan poised for a single instant, then leaped the low rail and plunged to the beach below. Charity heard it hit and then all grew still.

3

Charity jumped out of her car and raced across the road and down the steep path. Her breath came in sharp jerks in spite of her excellent physical condition. By the time she reached the overturned car, its wheels were still spinning. She barely glanced at it and ran to the crumpled figure in the sand, thrown clear of the car.

The girl was no older than Charity, pretty and pale, her face twisted in a ghastly expression. The smell of liquor confronted Charity when she bent closer to catch the faint whisper. "Guess I didn't make the curve."

"Where are you hurt?" Charity demanded through stiff lips. Never had she seen an accident except in silent films.

"All over."

Charity took in the grotesque position and bit back a cry of despair. Already the girl's eyes were growing dull and listless.

"Please, tell me what to do for you,"

Charity begged, but there was no response. The girl had lapsed into unconsciousness.

With unsteady fingers Charity began to explore tentatively. She discovered the girl must have landed against a large boulder that had smashed her body in several places.

Unnerved, Charity became aware of a low hum on the road above and began to scream for help. Seconds later uniformed police were around her, gently aiding the injured driver. Had they been following her, to get there so quickly?

"No use." One man put down the limp arm he'd been holding. "She's gone." He turned to Charity. "Did you see it happen?"

"Yes. She came toward me — I pulled over. She lost control of the car and was thrown out. She must not have had any — any brakes." She couldn't seem to stop babbling. "I tried to help her but I didn't know what to do."

"It wouldn't have done any good anyway," he reassured her, but to Charity's frenzied eyes it seemed the police officer avoided looking at her. Maybe he was lying. Maybe she could have helped. Maybe it was her fault the other girl was dead.

Gramps roared at her when she repeated her fears long after the tennis semifinals were played without her. He roared even louder when she defiantly announced, "Never again will I be in a place where if I'm needed I'll be helpless!" She thrust her chin forward in a remarkable imitation of his own determined profile. "I'm going to become a doctor or nurse or something, anything so I won't be useless!"

When he didn't answer, Charity pushed back her hair and looked across the room at him. He looked strange, almost ill. *"Jarvis!"* she screamed. The butler rushed in, took one look, and called Dr. Carlson.

A half-hour later the doctor left Gramps and came to the little sitting room where Charity waited, scared and guilty. He took both her hands in his and gently forced her to sit down, his eyes full of kindness. "He's fine, Charity. Has a bit of a tricky heart, but nothing to worry about."

She gasped with relief before a fresh fear hit her hard. "Tricky? Then it isn't something that will go away? Can't it be fixed?"

"I'm afraid not. Even the best doctor isn't God. I strongly suspect he may have had a touch of rheumatic fever as a boy." He smiled and her heart settled back in its normal place. "I can almost promise you he won't have trouble unless he's emotionally disturbed or terribly upset."

She felt his keen eyes rake over her before

he added, "You can be a great help by seeing he leads a happy, unruffled life. What's this about you wanting to study medicine? It seems to have upset Charles immensely."

She told him between sobs how she'd felt so useless, so unable to offer any assistance to the girl on the beach, how she'd decided she could never again be in such a hard place. "I want to be able to give," she finished simply.

"There are many ways to give, child. Not all of us will be doctors or nurses. Some will furnish money so others can study medicine."

"It isn't the same," she protested, still troubled over the day's events.

"Your place is to care for your grandfather." He ignored her sudden pulling back and stood. "Let that be your work if you feel you must be useful."

When he had gone Jarvis called her to see Gramps. He lay in the ancestral bed where he had been born and where he would in all probability die. It was the first time Charity could remember seeing him not fully dressed. Yet it didn't detract from his dignity. Gowned in a rich brocade robe, he sat propped against pillows. "Come here."

She avoided his eyes until she got to the

bed and then looked up. "I'm sorry, Gramps."

"It's all right. Carlson told you about my heart?"

"Yes." She nuzzled against his sleeve.

"No more talk of studying medicine?"

For a long moment she hesitated. Dreams of becoming worthy to meet life's crises died hard. But what choice did she have? "No, Gramps. I'll play nurse taking care of you." In spite of herself, a pang shot through her.

He was generous in victory. "And I won't insist on finishing school if you really want this other school."

She stared at him in amazement. "How did you — ?"

He chuckled. "I was called a few weeks ago. Since you won't be eighteen until next fall, the college felt it wise to check with me."

"You never said a word!" It was hard to believe he hadn't exploded when the call first came.

"Do you think I want you to be a puppet, leaping and dancing only when I pull the strings? Give me some credit. I may dictate but you have the right to make choices of your own, so long as I approve."

More than all the doctor's platitudes, Charles Endicott had shown he would really be all right. Charity left for her own room chastened and even a little amused. For hours she paced the floor. Had she been right to promise not to enter medicine? On the other hand, Gramps would work himself into a frenzy if she persisted with the idea. What would she gain learning to save lives if, because of it, she lost the dearest person on earth?

Over the summer her rebellion persisted, yet just when she was ready to announce she must study something other than how to become an intelligent millionaire, she'd see Gramps's overtired face and her personal declaration of independence would die on sealed lips. Sometimes they had long talks, during the trips to the White Mountains and Cape Cod or in the shadowy terrace of their own home.

"Our ancestors worked hard and were shrewd enough to invest. Now we have more than we can ever use. It's our responsibility to share." His keen gaze never left her face. "You'll be trained to differentiate between the ones who won't work and those who will benefit themselves and their country. God forbid we should ever again go through the hell of another war! But if we do, your generation will have to meet the challenges — and the losses."

Charity's eyes misted. Although some-what removed from the horrors of the world because of her grandfather and the peace of her home, patriotism burned within her. The November 1918 Armistice, and those who had fought to achieve it, loomed large in the young girl's life. One reason Cliff ap-pealed to her stemmed from his decorations for valor in the service of his country when his wealth could have bought another to go in his place.

Gramps continued. "Wealth can be a curse or a blessing. So can the aftermath of this war. Some have come home to find a speed-mad, all-for-freedom-and-self world. Shell-shocked, jobless, some turn to liquor to forget. Cricket, never drink."

Memory of the young girl and her over-turned car flooded Charity. "Never!" She watched the tipsy flight of a pollen-drunk bee. "Never, Gramps. I promise."

Charity stirred on her bench. It hadn't been easy being a teetotaler but she had kept her promise, even with Cliff, having nothing more riotous than fruit juices with sparkling soda. She'd never criticized his drinking; until today, he'd never been out of control.

Unhappiness swept through her. Even if Cliff recovered, could they ever hope to make a success of their marriage? Why had she been so infuriated with the way he had taken possession of her? The ring on her finger gave him the right, didn't it?

She twisted it in the moonlight, watching it glint. Some of its bright sparkle had dimmed, the way her ideal of Cliff had become a little tarnished.

"This is ridiculous," she whispered to the night. "Just because he didn't act as respectfully as I always want him to shouldn't mean anything. It's my fault if I set my standards so high no man could ever live up to them! Even Gramps says men are different, in spite of all the postwar freedom. I guess I just wanted a companion as well as a lover." Regret crept into her heart. "If I'd just told him how I feel about drinking and explained why! I know he loves me. After this tragedy he'll probably see what can happen and maybe even decide it just isn't worth it. Then we can be happy again."

The same thrill that had filled her when Cliff singled her out at the Christmas cotillion months before cooled her warm face and settled her troubled mind. Gramps had said everything would be better in the morning. She had to believe that. Charity gathered the hooded garment closer, tucked her feet beneath her, and let herself drift into the past. Gradually the happy memories replaced the indelibly etched scene of the broken plane and Cliff's pleading eyes. She watched as dawn sent an exploring finger into the sky. She saw how it became encouraged with what it found and sent other ambassadors to greet the day. A lovely pinkish light bathed the garden. A robin stirred. The early morning hush soon became a concert hall.

Entranced, Charity listened and didn't move a muscle. It had been years since she had been up and alone at this time of day. Even the luxurious camping trips were in laughing, chattering groups, making the chance of seeing and hearing something like this impossible.

"When Cliff is well I'll tell him we'll go ahead and get married," she resolved. "I'll also tell him I don't want any fancy honeymoon with a million people around. Maybe we can find some forgotten place and enjoy at least for a time beauty like this."

Not until she heard stirring in the servants' quarters did Charity reluctantly gather herself together and go back to the house. What would Long Island think if they knew she'd spent the entire night on a bench in the garden? A gaminlike grin transformed her perfect features and she nodded solemnly to the sun stretching and peering over the horizon. "I won't tell if you won't." She waved and ran lightly inside, feeling as if she had returned from a long journey.

For several days news from the hospital in the city was guarded. Cliff was still listed as critical. Charity alternated between periods of hope and black despair. Again guilt crushed down on her. A dozen times she thought aloud, "If I'd gone on when I wanted to and learned about medicine, it could have made the difference." It became a fixation with her. She felt she was leaving girlhood behind forever, becoming old before she had had the chance to finish being young. She'd been given a second chance to redeem herself — and had again been unprepared.

She grew pale and listless. Friends didn't help. When they came, they either didn't mention Cliff at all, except with veiled glances, or they wanted to know every gruesome detail of the crash, her feelings, and what she thought Cliff's chances were. She finally told Jarvis just to tell them she wasn't home. "It won't be a lie," she told him. "I'm not at home to them. Even those who mean well can't understand."

One evening after a particularly trying day Charity and Gramps sat in the garden, surrounded by loveliness — and discouragement. The hospital report had been noncommital but she heard in the carefully cheerful voice little hope. "Tomorrow's a long time coming, Gramps."

He didn't pretend to misunderstand. "I know." His gray eyes reflected lights from the softly glowing water that had snatched some color from the setting sun. "Cricket, when this is all over, let's go away somewhere."

She read the truth in his face. "He isn't going to get better, is he?"

"No." He gave her the unvarnished fact. "If he were going to rally it would have been before now." Pain creased his forehead. "You have the right to know."

"Thanks, Gramps." She knew she was dead white when she bowed her head. So Cliff would die after all, leaving her to wonder forever if she could have saved him.

"Don't go on blaming yourself." Gramps leaned forward and looked at her intently.

"How can I help it?" She bit her lips to stop their trembling. "He loved me, trusted me. He asked me for help and I wasn't able to give it."

The sun slid out of sight as if unwilling to witness the shadows over the garden.

"I'm just an ornament," Charity continued brokenly. "If Cliff had lived, I'd have graced his home. Like his silver cups won at sports events and his shining crystal and silver. Pretty, maybe, but how useful?" She spread out her beautiful hands. "Hunt's hands are brown and worn from polishing cars and working on them. Our cook's hands are strong from honest work. But my hands —"

"Stop it, Charity!" Anger crept into her grandfather's eyes. "I've had enough of this feeling sorry for yourself."

She felt as if he had slapped her. "Sorry for *myself?* That's the worst thing you've ever said to me. It's Cliff I feel sorry for, don't you understand? And that girl when I was seventeen. And anyone who happens to ever need help if I'm the only person around." Her ragged voice shattered the peace of the descending twilight.

Before she could continue a well-modulated voice said, "Begging your pardon, Mr. Endicott, but there's a call." Jarvis broke off.

"From the hospital?" Charity was on her feet. Even before Jarvis could nod, she had started toward the house. "I'll take it." She could hear Jarvis explaining, "The person insisted on speaking to one of you personally."

56

The path past roses shaking their fragrance against her skirt as she brushed by seemed endless. Then up a few steps and into the hall. "Hello?"

"Miss Endicott?"

Charity caught her breath. She hadn't been called that since she graduated. "Yes?"

"I'm sorry to inform you that Mr. Cliff Marshall died about an hour ago. You left instructions to let you know."

Charity's fingers tightened on the phone. "Thank you for calling." Her voice was as impersonal as the one that had come with the long-expected news. She turned. Gramps stood a few feet away, his face wrinkling in sympathy. He started toward her.

"No, Gramps. I have to handle this on my own." She hated the hurt she saw in his eyes but didn't relent. Instead she took a long, deep breath and marched upstairs.

There was no haven from what she had somehow known would happen. A second phone call came. First Cliff's best friend, then another and another. Through them all Charity quietly and efficiently persevered, frozen on the outside, bleeding in her heart. Cliff, gone forever? Impossible! It was all a nightmare, something to be endured until it ended and he bounded into the hall. Things would be better in the morning. There could be nothing worse than Cliff dying, could there?

Before she regained solid footing from Cliff's death, new problems arose to mock her. No one seemed to know anything about Cliff's relatives or whom to contact. Newspapers had made a circus of his death with headlines shouting to the world:

MYSTERIOUS MILLIONAIRE DIES IN PLANE CRASH. WHERE DID HE COME FROM? WHO WAS HE? FIANCÉE INCOMMUNICADO.

Speculative accounts followed, giving Cliff Marshall's death undue importance; was Cliff a highly respected scion or a foreign spy?

"Sometimes I wonder if I can stand it," Charity told Gramps after he finally showed her the papers. "Since we were the most closely connected, I guess it's up to us to make the decisions about the funeral, burial, and so on." She gritted her teeth. "Anything, Gramps, just so it's private. And don't let any reporters near me or I'll throw something!"

At last it was over. At least Charity thought it was.

She was wrong. A formal investigation into the crash had to be held. Since Charity had been the only witness, there was no way she could avoid appearing. Gramps swore and threatened. It did no good. The investigator seemed determined to discover exactly what caused the crash. In the prehearing meeting Charity had the distinct feeling the man disliked anyone with money and planned to prove something because of it, but she didn't know what.

She chose a simple navy suit, white blouse, and navy shoes. Her only jewelry was her engagement ring, now unspeakably heavy on her left hand. Gramps smiled at her when she was called to speak and she aimed a glance of gratitude toward him.

"Miss Endicott, you were with Cliffton Marshall the day of the accident?"

The words didn't chill her as much as the investigator's steely stare. The small, impersonal room, with its drab brown walls interrupted only by an American flag, threatened to close in around her. She moistened her lips. "Yes."

"Your relationship to the deceased was?"

The deceased. How cold and inadequate for the laughing man Cliff had been! "We were engaged to be married."

"I see." The man drummed his fingertips

59

on a small table. "You quarreled that afternoon?"

How did he know that? "Yes. He'd been drinking. I didn't want to fly with him."

"That tallies with what the waiter at the restaurant reported."

Resentment boiled up inside Charity. Her eyes blazed. "Why shouldn't it? It's the truth!"

A sardonic smile crossed her persecutor's face. "And can you tell us just what happened after you left the restaurant?"

"We drove to the field. Cliff insisted on flying." Stark horror returned, as strong and insidious as it had been when it happened. "He wanted me to go. I said no — I drove a little way off." She gazed past the investigator, past Gramps, out the open window. "He took off although I tried to stop him. When he came in for a landing, I ran to the field and tried to wave him down."

"You *what?*" Twin coals glowed in the investigator's face. "You actually ran in front of a pilot attempting to land?"

"He was too low." It sounded weak in the emotion-filled room.

"Sir," Gramps was on his feet, hair waving wildly. "May I remind you my granddaughter is not on trial here?"

Charity choked back an appreciative,

"Good for you, Gramps!"

"She may very well be put on trial. If it can be proven she deliberately caused the accident, that because she was in the way Cliffton Marshall swerved and crashed, then it was her fault. As his fiancée, your granddaughter is presumably heir to what will obviously prove to be a substantial fortune."

Charity turned to stone. He was — was he — accusing her of *murder?*

"By all that's holy," Gramps had started forward, "you'll be sued for slander if it's the last thing I do!" He lifted the heavy walking stick in his hand, prepared to do physical battle.

"Stop, Gramps!" Charity sprang toward him, grabbed the stick, and forced it to the floor. Panting, she turned to the investigating board. "Cliff Marshall crashed and died because he had been drinking too much. The waiter will substantiate what he was served. You can take my word for the rest," her scornful eyes raked the silent trio. "Or if that isn't good enough, the ambulance helpers from the first hospital he was taken to will prove what I say. I came here because it seemed the right thing to do. Now my grandfather and I are leaving — and you can be sure our lawyers will contact you."

The tallest of the men stood. "Miss Endicott, I apologize." He sent a furious glance at the chief investigator. "The only excuse I can offer is that sometimes one gets carried away in the zeal of discovering what causes plane crashes. I hope you'll accept this and let the lawsuit go. I'm fully satisfied, as I am sure my colleagues are," he said as he stared at the investigator until the man looked down. "I'm sure you don't want any more unpleasant publicity as we certainly do not. In fact, there may be a change in the investigation task force soon."

Charity was too tired to care. "Come on, Gramps, let's go." Fighting the urge to let her bones turn to jelly, she took his arm and walked out, head high. But once in the car and safe from prying eyes and the inevitable, persistent reporters who had caught them outside the building, she wilted. "Isn't it *ever* going to end?"

"It's over, Cricket. I promise you that." The stern set of Charles Endicott's jaw relaxed when she leaned against his shoulder. "Tomorrow we'll talk about getting away. Somewhere where no one will know or care that you are Charity Endicott, *the* Charity Endicott who had planned to marry Cliff Marshall."

Nerves that had been taut as guitar

strings slowly relaxed.

"Can you think of anywhere you'd like to go?" Gramps took advantage of her small smile.

Visions of resorts, beaches, and European cities danced and receded in her over-worked mind. She gazed unseeingly out the window beyond buildings grasping for the sky. "I think I'd like to leave Charity Endicott on Long Island and go where a girl called Cricket can learn how to start all over again."

"I know the exact place."

"Really?" Charity looked at him with more interest than she'd felt she could ever again show in anything.

"Yes." Grim satisfaction lit up the worn face for a minute. "We'll talk about it in the morning."

4

Charity stood at her window and watched as the summer sun shot rays into the quiet garden. Early as it was, she felt rested for the first time since the tragedy. No tossing and turning had kept her awake; Gramps's promise that the nightmare had ended fanned a flicker of hope. When Gramps made a promise, he kept it.

She smiled and let herself look at the future. Her wish from the night before shimmered in the still air. . . . *leave Charity Endicott on Long island . . . go where a girl called Cricket can learn to start all over again.*

Gramps's words. *I know the exact place. We'll talk about it in the morning.*

"I even feel like Cricket," she told the dew-fresh morning. She flung her arms wide. "Free and able to go on with life."

A half-hour later she raced down the beautiful stairway. "Gramps?"

"In here, Cricket."

She followed his voice to the library,

started to speak, and halted at the expression on his face. How old he looked! How serious. Fear gnawed at her heart. He had held up so well through their ordeal. Surely he wouldn't become ill now when things looked brighter.

"Close the door, please."

His hoarse voice released her from a statuelike pose. The great door swung shut and the girl slowly crossed to the massive desk that dominated the room.

"Sit down, Cricket." Faded eyes that could still burn gazed into her troubled face. "You know I never break a promise?"

A fresh wave of fear roiled over her. "Yes."

"And that I promised this whole thing was truly over?"

She moistened her lips and nodded but words stopped back in her throat.

Charles Endicott's shoulders slumped. "Something has come up. . . ." Pain contorted his features. "You have to be strong."

"What is it? You're not worse, are you?" A sob tore through her choked throat. "That's the only thing I couldn't stand."

"No, no, I'm fine. Haven't felt so good for ages. Finer than frog hair and that's pretty fine." He managed a grin that hid none of his turmoil and did little to help Cricket except to relieve her anxiety over his health.

"I can handle it, Gramps," she promised and leaned forward. Her long, beautiful hair shone against the whiteness of her simple morning gown.

He sat erect. "Just a few moments ago I received a strange telephone call. A woman, asking, no, demanding, an audience with us both as soon as possible."

"Who on earth —" Cricket's eyes opened wide.

A world of tenderness underscored her grandfather's next words. "She says her name is Mrs. Cliff Marshall."

"Impossible!" The walls of the library closed in on her and Cricket forced herself to take a deep breath.

"That's what I told her." Gramps spread his hands in defeat. "She claims she has solid proof. She also says if we don't see her the newspapers will. I told her to come here at ten o'clock and God help her if she breathed a word of this to anyone else before then."

He reached across the desk and grasped Cricket's hand. She felt the strength on which she had relied since childhood. His bushy brows came together and he looked deep into her eyes. "You have an almost un-canny way of discerning the truth. You in-herited it from me. Between us we can tell if

66

there's any truth to this story . . . if it's just a sordid attempt at blackmail triggered by all the publicity about Cliff's little-known past."

She clutched his hand, steadied her reeling senses, and arrogantly raised her chin until the resemblance between them surfaced. "I'll know." She bit back an hysterical laugh and forced herself to add, "In the meantime we'd better get to the breakfast table. You know what a tyrant Cook can be, especially if she's made an omelet or popovers."

Color stole back into Gramps's face and he crushed her hand until she wondered if the bones would crack. Then he released her and rose, gallantly offering his arm to escort her to the sunny breakfast room.

It can't be happening. It isn't true. Over and over the disbelief attacked Cricket as she made a pretense of enjoying lighter than air popovers that stuck in her throat and enormous ruby strawberries still on their hulls ready to be dipped in sugar. Only the steaming chocolate slid down easily and fortified her for the ten o'clock deadline. Gramps kept up a running commentary on world events, neighbors' doings, and deceived no one. The clock in the hall striking ten came as a relief; the punctual pronouncement of the doorbell soon followed.

Jarvis entered the breakfast room. "A la— a woman to see you both, sir. She says she has an appointment but refuses to give her name." Outraged dignity covered every inch of the perturbed butler's face.

"It's all right. She's expected." Gramps flung down his monogrammed napkin and rose. "Show her into my study in five minutes."

"Very well, sir." Any curiosity on Jarvis's part stayed masked and he vanished in his usual measured tread.

"Let her sit in the entry hall for a few minutes and we'll have the advantage of being in the study first," Gramps observed.

Cricket couldn't restrain a nervous giggle. "Gramps, you're magnificent."

"Of course. I'm Charles Endicott." She tucked her hand under his arm and laughed again.

Cricket held her breath once they settled into the businesslike study so in contrast with the rest of the house. Jarvis's slow tread and the softer steps of the unknown claimant sent shivers playing tag on her spine.

Jarvis opened the study door and announced, "Your visitor, sir," and discreetly withdrew, closing the door behind him.

Prepared to discover a cheap, overdressed woman obviously out for money, Cricket gasped and Gramps let out a "Harrumph."

The girl who stood braced against the doorway, obviously terrified, fit none of their expectations. Mrs. Cliff Marshall, if Cliff had really married her, resembled more than anything a defenseless chick separated from its mother. Frightened blue eyes as honest as any Cricket had ever seen peered from beneath blond bangs. More blond hair tumbled to the shoulders of a neat but worn black suit. Carefully mended gloves hung limply from one hand. Immaculate grooming couldn't hide the telltale signs of poverty that clung to her like a needy child.

"Mr. Endicott? Miss Endicott?" The frail girl swayed and righted herself with a bitter laugh. "You probably think a faint is next on my program. It isn't. I've been ill." A little color tinted her parchment-shaded face.

"What's your name, child?" Gramps's question hung in the air.

"Mary. Mary Marshall. May I sit down?"

Cricket could scarcely believe the soft voice, as well modulated as her own.

"Please do." Gramps stood and indicated a chair, a courtesy that told Cricket he was

69

experiencing the same feelings that pulled at her.

"I want to apologize for, for threatening to talk to the newspapers," the girl said. Shame filled her eyes. "I didn't know another way to make sure you would see me. I'm not a blackmailer."

Cricket believed her and yet — "Then why . . . ?"

"Why did I come?" Mary's sad eyes confirmed her story. "Not for myself. I'd rather starve." She fumbled in her handbag. "It's for him." She slid a picture from the bag and handed it to Cricket.

A laughing, light-haired child stared up at her. A child unmistakably Cliff's, bearing the same expression Cricket had seen so often when he cajoled her into some new venture. She wordlessly passed it on to Gramps.

"You have proof?" Gramps's brows almost met.

"I do." She fumbled in her bag again and produced a sheaf of evidence. "Marriage certificate, three years ago. My son's birth certificate, two years ago. A sworn statement by the pastor of my church in California."

"All before we met Cliff," Gramps admitted.

"If you want to have your attorneys examine them, you may." Mary leaned her head against the high chair back, swallowed convulsively, and closed her eyes for a minute.

"That won't be necessary," Cricket burst out in a moment of generosity while her final dreams about Cliff went up in flames.

"Thank you. You, sir?" She turned to Charles.

He glanced at Cricket, caught her brief nod, and handed back the documents. "Do you want to tell us about it? And what you want of us?"

A spasm crossed the pale face but Mary Marshall remained stoic. "I loved Cliffton Marshall from the time I was a little girl, although he was years older. During the war I prayed and lived for the day he'd come back. I never even looked at another boy. Well, the war ended. He came home, hero to the town and me. Later he noticed I'd grown up and eventually we married. By then he'd begun to get established by speculating and he was having incredible luck. He also began to grow away from me. All I ever wanted was a home and family and husband. Cliff wanted more. When he found out a baby was on the way he disappeared."

"The hound!" Gramps reared up in his chair.

71

Mary smiled what Cricket knew must be the saddest smile in the world. Indignation at the way she'd been treated effectively extinguished her last romantic feelings for Cliff.

"I had no close family." Mary's lips trembled. "Our pastor and his wife were wonderful, especially when word came that Cliff had gone to Mexico and somehow used wealth and position to divorce me."

What a rotter Cliff had been! One look at Gramps's thundercloud countenance showed his concurring feelings.

"I believe once two people have been joined by God nothing can change that. When I saw your picture in the paper I wrote to Cliffton and told him he must tell you about me and about his son." Her blue eyes filled with tears when she looked directly at Cricket. "You didn't look to me like the kind of girl who would want a second-hand husband."

Cricket winced. "I wouldn't," she confirmed, hands clenched. "If I'd known. . . ." Her voice died yet her conscience accused: *Didn't you? What about the times you shoved back those little doubts? And the way you felt when he practically manhandled you that last afternoon?*

"How can we help you, Mary?" Gramps

quietly asked. "Do you need money?"

"Yes." Her simple answer elevated Cricket's respect for her. "Doctors have told me I must have time to rest. I can't support Barney."

"Is that your son's name?"

"Yes, after my brother, Barney Delevan. He should have been Cliffton, Jr., but I couldn't bear that."

Cricket couldn't believe the lack of bitterness in Mary's words. "He acted so rotten. He — don't you hate him?" Her words ran together.

"No." The blue eyes softened. "Jesus says we're to forgive our enemies as He forgives us when we do wrong. It took me a long time. Now all I feel is pity for the way he died without knowing Christ."

If Cricket's life had depended on it, she couldn't have forced one word past the lump of admiration that swelled inside her. What Cliff had done to Mary surpassed his sins to Cricket a million times. How could the young widow sit there without condemnation when Cricket wanted to scream at Cliff for violating even his memory?

Mary turned back to Charles. "I thought you'd know the best way to do things. I know Cliff had at least some assets — a car, bank account. If you could see we got them

without a lot of publicity and court proce-
dures, they'd help raise Barney. I vow to you
I will never take anything for myself except
to help me get strong enough to work. Once
I do, I will pay back every penny and it will
be in trust for my son — and Cliff's."

"That wouldn't be necessary." Gramps
reached for a snowy handkerchief and blew
his nose loudly.

Mary leaned forward and her eyes
glowed. "Sir, if you were in my place,
wouldn't you do the same?"

Cricket wanted to shout, "Bravo!" Instead, she reached for her own handkerchief
when her grandfather started to speak.

"Yes, Mary." As if regretting the emotion
in his voice he continued, "Just one thing. I
intend to make you a generous allowance so
you can concentrate on mending." He
raised one domineering hand to still her au-
tomatic protest.

"Mary, your coming here has been a great
shock. Yet it will be the very thing that helps
my granddaughter heal, perhaps more than
anything else on earth."

"But I don't want payment for that," she
cried. Flags of color flew in her thin cheeks.

"You need the money, you've already said
so. Don't let pride keep you from taking it."
Charles cleared his throat and dropped his

74

voice several notes. "That God you believe in. You expect Him to look after you, don't you?"

She nodded but looked bewildered. "I don't see what that has to do with it."

"Mary, that same God has blessed the Endicotts abundantly, far more than we'll ever need. If you don't want to accept help from us, won't you accept it from your God, who after all owns the entire world and its wealth?"

Cricket's mouth dropped open. Gramps, talking like that? When had he ever expressed such sentiments? Oh, he often talked about the responsibility of the rich to the less fortunate but the idea that God entered into the situation had certainly never been discussed. Or had Mary's forgiving spirit and witness to the power of Jesus inspired Gramps?

"If you put it that way, I cannot refuse," Mary said.

Cricket, following an impulse strange to her cool nature, slipped from her chair and knelt in front of the girl with blue shadows under her eyes. "Mary, sometime could we see little Barney?"

"I have a better idea." Gramps's usual keen grasp of what needed to be done rose over the clasp of the girls' hands and Mary's

75

nod. He positively beamed. "Where's that little guy of yours right now?"

"Why, in California. With my minister and his wife. They want to sort of adopt us but he isn't highly paid and they have children of their own."

"Good, good," Charles trumpeted. "Then there's no reason why you can't accept a job here, is there?"

Every trace of color fled Mary's face. She stared at Charles as if he'd suddenly gone berserk. "Sir?"

"My daughter and I are planning an extended vacation. We need someone to live here and supervise the staff," he said blandly.

Cricket bit her lip to keep back a smile. Jarvis and Hunt and the rest of the long-term staff were more than capable of caring for the Endicott mansion no matter how long the master and mistress were absent.

"You don't mean you want Barney and me to actually *live* here?" Mary gasped even while a tiny flare of hope brightened her eyes. "It's impossible."

A moment later she added, "What would people say? Your friends, Long Island society?"

"Our *friends* will be happy to welcome a brave girl and her beautiful son," Charles told her. "I don't care two feathers about the rest of them." His casual wave dismissed the others and their possible gossip.

"What about you, Miss Endicott?" Mary's words pinned Cricket to the wall.

For a moment the dark-eyed girl thought of the storm of whispers and innuendo. If Mary quietly went elsewhere, perhaps the papers would fail to get the story. If she came here — Cricket inwardly shuddered at the field day reporters would have. No wonder Cliff had hated publicity!

A second later Cricket chastised herself for such cowardice. Even though she was innocent of deliberately contributing to an impossible situation, Cliff had involved her. If she'd been more insistent on learning who and what he was and less flattered by his attentions, or if she'd had some kind of training. . . . The question now had nothing to do with her inadequacies and everything to do with two more innocent persons. Would she let publicity keep her from doing what deep inside she had felt was right ever since Gramps suggested the plan?

Through a haze she smiled at Mary. "We'll be glad, no, proud, to have you live in our home with your son — for as long as you wish," she added in a final capitulation and tribute to the young mother's courage.

For the first time, Mary crumpled. Years of trouble behind her, she put her hands in her lap and sobbed. In the face of such genuine feeling Cricket and Gramps could only avert their gazes and wait for the storm to pass. When it did, Mary lifted a radiant, swollen face and whispered, "You are so good. I didn't want to come. I had to. But I never expected this."

I won't let her down, Cricket fiercely vowed. *No matter how hard it is to face others.*

An hour later, driven by Hunt in the limousine, Mary left to get her few things from the modest room that was all she could afford. Cricket faced Gramps. "Well?"

"I've never been prouder of you than today," he said. "Now, would you mind telling Cook we'll have a guest for lunch and see that a room is made ready?" His lips tightened and his smile turned wintry. "I have some business with the newspapers. Hmmm, remember that young fellow I financed at college? Wouldn't be a bit surprised if he'd like a real scoop. Can you take it?"

"If Mary Delevan Marshall can go through what she has and come out without bitterness, even forgiving Cliff, I can take it," Cricket said resolutely. "Just — Gramps — why are you breaking the story?"

"Best way in the world." His shrewd glance reassured her. "If we try and hide things, someone, sometime, will unearth the story according to their viewpoint. Defang the rattler and the venom is distilled — in this case society's buzzing will be at least partially stilled."

Cricket managed what passed for a laugh but when the following news story came out she applauded both Gramps and David Barrington, whose byline appeared.

FINAL CHAPTER IN MARSHALL STORY

A surprise ending marks *finis* to the supposed mystery surrounding Cliff Marshall, who recently died as a result of an earlier plane crash on Long Island. It has been learned from the most reliable source of all — Mr. Charles Endicott, grandfather of Charity Endicott, Mr. Marshall's fiancée — that Marshall's former wife Mary and her two-year-old son Barney will be permanent guests of the Endicotts at the Endicott family mansion.

Cliffton Marshall obtained a divorce in Mexico some time before coming to Long Island. Endicott states in his usual, down-to-earth manner, "Folks can't always tell about other folks, can they?" It is assumed this refers to the former marriage and that Miss Endicott had been unaware of same. However, the continuing presence of Mary and Barney Marshall with the Endicotts should erase unpleasant speculation on the part of those who engage in such. Charles Endicott reports the two new additions to his household are now members of the family and he expects them to be welcomed by Long Island friends and neighbors.

While Charity Endicott was not available for an interview, a signed statement from her endorses her grandfather's sentiments completely. A luncheon for intimate acquaintances and friends in honor of Mary and Barney Marshall will be arranged once the child arrives from California and is settled in the Endicott home.

"Gramps, you're incorrigible. Did you really say that about folks not being able to tell about other folks?"

"Why not?" Aggrieved innocence mingled with a twinkle in the watching eyes. "What *I* like is the way young Barrington wrote some pretty strong statements into the facts." He rattled his copy of the paper. "Look here," he pointed. ". . . *continuing presence . . . should erase unpleasant speculation. . . .*" He threw back his head and laughed louder than he had for months. "It implies that those 'who engage in such' had jolly well not be speculating, huh?"

Gramps lowered the paper. "You know even this won't squelch all the gossip."

"I know." Cricket caught her lower lip in her teeth. She crossed to the window and looked out. "When I start feeling sorry for myself I think of Mary, alone, waiting for a baby that had been deserted by its father." She broke off.

"It's sad that just maybe the best thing Cliff Marshall did since coming home from serving his country was to die."

"*Gramps!*" Cricket whirled, not trusting her own ears. "That's a terrible epitaph for a life."

"I didn't write it, Cricket. He did." Gramps didn't back down one bit; he just sat there looking at her.

"I don't understand how you can say such a thing," she protested. "I'm still angry with Cliff but even Mary has forgiven him, and he's dead. Isn't that enough?"

Gramps sighed. "Yes, he's dead, leaving a frail wife to fend for herself and a small son. What if he hadn't died? How long could Mary Marshall push herself or accept help from an already overburdened minister and his family? You heard her say she believes marriage is for life. She couldn't remarry as long as Cliff lived because she doesn't see divorce as valid. Don't get me wrong, Cricket. I wouldn't wish Cliff or anyone else dead, no matter what they'd done. On the other hand, since it happened, you're free and so is Mary. What if you and Cliff had married and you discovered Mary and Barney's existence?"

She hadn't really considered it. "I don't know."

Gramps crossed his arms on his chest so that he looked like a benevolent judge. "After time passes some smart fellow will take a look at Mary and Barney and see their worth." He stroked his chin. "Far be it from me to play matchmaker, but our young reporter friend, David Barrington, is in his late twenties. How about asking him to dinner?"

"*After* Mary gets back from the West Coast with Barney, of course," Cricket mocked.

"Of course." Gramps acted surprised and

82

didn't fool Cricket at all.

"You old fraud. Don't you know it's dangerous business to try and play God?"

If her accusation disturbed Gramps, he didn't let on. Instead he shot back, "Well, Mary's first marriage sure wasn't made in heaven. Remember, marriage has to be lived on earth." He grinned wickedly. "And if I can help the Almighty with a gentle nudge here and there in the right direction, I aim to do it!"

Cricket couldn't help laughing. Yet even as she did, a foreboding sense of warning chilled her. Why did Gramps's comments bother her? His "helping the Almighty" with Mary's problems had turned out all right so far. She hoped her ominous feelings were simply that, nothing more . . . especially now when her world had just begun to right itself.

5

David Barrington's cleverly worded news-paper account killed much of the gossip about the new additions to the Endicott family. Raised eyebrows lowered in a hurry. Once Charles Endicott took a stand, Long Island society bowed to the inevitable.

The night before Cricket and her grandfather planned to depart, they held a dinner party to launch Mary into the neighborhood. "Get her accepted before we leave," Gramps had advised. "Otherwise a few snobs and jealous mamas who coveted Cliff for their daughters may make Mary unhappy while we're gone."

Cricket adjusted a flounce of her pale yellow dress and smiled warmly at Mary. "Well?"

Tears threatened to spill from eyes that matched the cornflower blue gown Cricket had insisted on purchasing for her along with a wealth of other pretty but more practical clothes. "If anyone had told me a few weeks ago I'd be here —" she gestured around the beautiful drawing room — "I'd have thought that person demented."

A pang shot through Cricket. In spite of the loving care Mary and her son Barney had received since Mary came back from California, she remained frail. "You promise not to do too much while we're gone?"

"As if I could find enough to do except care for Barney." Mary's tears disappeared and a tremulous smile hovered on her sensitive mouth. "It's almost like God didn't have me wait for Heaven. To be here, I mean."

Cricket caught the approving look David Barrington quickly covered. Gramps's kindly meddling had included David in their daily life until he also seemed part of the family. His rather shy manner put Mary at ease and Cricket could just see a happily-ever-after ending for Mary and Barney sometime in the future.

She sighed. Any prospect of the same for herself seemed remote. If she couldn't judge character any better than she had judged Cliff, she'd better not trust men at all. Rebellion stirred within her. Not for Cliff, for that had ended with Mary's arrival. But when Barney Marshall held out chubby two-year-old arms and Cricket picked up the laughing little boy for the first time, she ached inside.

Did Mary sense her feelings? Perhaps. In any event, she quietly said, "Everything I went through with Cliff was worth it to have Barney." The look she sent her small son made Cricket's arms tighten protectively in understanding.

Only one event had marred Mary and Barney's stay so far. The morning before the scheduled dinner party Mary broke the seal of a note, read it and gasped.

"What is it, child?" Gramps laid his fork down on the immaculate breakfast table cloth and drew his brows together.

"My brother. He wants to come here."

Cricket glanced at Gramps in surprise. Mary certainly didn't seem happy about it. He shrugged.

Mary struggled to express herself. "He's — it sounds harsh to say — but Barney isn't a good person. When we were smaller I idolized him but something happened to him." She frowned. "When he came home from France the Barney I adored had turned into a totally different person. I don't know if it came from being at the front but all he cares about now is himself." Her blue eyes pleaded with them for understanding.

"You think he wants something now?"
Gramps cut straight to the heart of Mary's
misery.

She nodded. "He always does. He said h
could have been killed and his country
doesn't care about him now that people
have put away the flags from Armistice Day
He's callous and he uses people." She
sighed. "It's so hard to believe a person
could change that much."

"Invite him to the dinner," Gramps told
her. "He's your brother, no matter what.
Some men react to war one way, some another." He cocked his head to one side. "It
might be just as well to let him know you'll
be here permanently. Will he want money?"

Instead of answering, Mary hesitated.
Hot color filled her face. "Could — would
you — may I tell him things aren't all settled
yet and that while I'm living here you're
caring for Barney and me but —" she broke
off.

Gramps studied her downcast face. "If
you like I won't issue your wages for a time. I
can bank them for you. Mary, I've already
made arrangements for you to shop at our
favorite stores and have put your name on
record. That way you'll have what you need
but only control limited cash."

Cricket could feel the other girl's relief

and when dapper, dark-haired Barney Delevan arrived punctually for dinner the next night Cricket could see why. He bore no resemblance to either Mary or his namesake. His curious trick of raising one eyebrow and twitching his small dark mustache left her cold. His flattering, "No wonder you took in my poor sister and nephew — I can see you're as beautiful inside as out," earned a freezing, "How nice you could come" before Cricket turned to someone else. David Barrington positively hovered around Mary and only after dinner did Barney get a chance at his sister. Cricket noticed her apprehension, Barney's low conversation, and Mary's quick headshake. She also noted the way the man's lips tightened and his quickly concealed anger. Would Barney haunt Mary while she and Gramps were gone?

"I wouldn't worry about her," Gramps whispered in her ear. "Mary Delevan Marshall is a lot tougher than she looks. See what she's already gone through. That God of hers is really something. When we get back, whenever that is, I want Mary to tell us more about her amazing faith."

A strange longing for the peace she often saw in Mary crept into Cricket's now empty heart. Between the recent revelations and the continuing guilt over her own helplessness Cricket hadn't returned to normal. Could Mary's God be the answer?

A burst of music from well-trained musicians cut short her introspection yet somewhere a seed lay buried, waiting for time and the right conditions to help it mature.

"When we get back" sounded vague and faraway. Right now all Cricket wanted was the chance to get away.

Several days earlier Cricket had encountered Gramps in his study. Out of the blue he had asked, "How would you like to go to Wyoming?"

"*Wyoming!* What's there?" Cricket stared.

"The doctor says it would do me good to get away from Long Island, the East, everything that might remind me of business. I know you don't want to head for Europe or any place you might be recognized. Doc knows of a working cattle ranch that has begun taking in guests. There's clean air, good food, and riding." A sparkle filled his tired old eyes.

Cricket couldn't remember when he'd shown enthusiasm like this. He usually just worked and worked except when they stole off for vacations. Now he acted like a kid before Christmas.

"Yes." Memories filled his eyes. "When your grandmother and I married we had little money but we managed to get in a brief honeymoon in the Grand Teton Mountains. We always meant to go back, but. . . ."

Cricket mentally finished the sentence. *You got too busy.* You discovered money and made it your god. You piled it up and then Grandma died and my folks died and it was too late.

Her sudden insight gentled her voice. "I wish no one knew me out there."

"Why should they? Our middle names are both Lee. We're registered as Charles and Cricket Lee."

"You knew I'd go all the time, didn't you?" She rubbed her cheek against his rough tweed coat sleeve.

"You're so much like your grandmother. That's why I made them call you Cricket," he reminded her for the umpteenth time.

"When do we go?"

"The day after Mary's party."

"How?"

"By train, private car, of course."

Cricket couldn't help accusing, "Your idea of roughing it, I take?"

"I'm sure you'll find things rough enough on a working cattle ranch to suit you," he said dryly. He added, "Cricket, you know how I love your long dark hair but if you really want to keep from being recognized you might consider getting it cut." Cricket's dark eyes opened wide. The few times she'd suggested such a thing Gramps acted like she'd committed a mortal sin even thinking it.

The next morning the well-styled cap of short, dark curls justified the decision. Sometimes she felt like the young Cricket she had been, light and carefree. She'd never realized how much difference a change of hairstyle could make in her attitude.

After a tearful farewell to Mary and Barney, a limousine deposited them at the station and Charles and Cricket Lee began their journey into anonymity. Cricket's love of needling — "How anyone can be anonymous in their own private railroad car is beyond me" — continued to delight Gramps. From mountains to rolling, fertile valleys to endless cornfields and dusty barrenness, Cricket felt Charity Endicott disappearing and Cricket Lee emerging.

With his usual shrewdness, Gramps had them leave his private railroad car long before reaching their destination so they could arrive like other tourists. Cricket couldn't take her gaze off the foothills that rose into the whitecapped Grand Teton Range, part of the mighty Rocky Mountains. Cattle grazed in knee-deep grass near streams and rivers. Tillicum Ranch lay near the mighty Snake River at the very foot of the Tetons, Gramps explained. Taking on guests kept the ranch going during harsh seasons and when stock prices lowered.

Cricket never forgot her first view of Tillicum Ranch, an Indian name that meant "friend." Her untrained, excited mind had expected an Old West buckboard to meet them at the station, complete with cowboy, red bandanna, and horses. The comfortable touring car and respectful driver whose only concession to western style lay in his big hat and worn boots were a definite letdown.

Tillicum Ranch, sprung from a homestead, more than made up for the transportation. A log lodge, outbuildings, and a few private cabins, also log, grew against the foothill background as if they'd been created there. Long-eared rabbits the driver called "jacks" stared at the travelers with bulging eyes. Two deer slowly crossed the well-defined road and mingled with red and white cattle and varicolored horses.

"Perfect!" Cricket exclaimed as Gramps patted her hand. The driver grinned until his smile looked like a crack in a cheap watermelon. "Glad you like it, folks. We do, too."

Towering evergreens dwarfed the buildings. Split-log corrals restrained wild horses.

"Look!" Cricket's elbow dug into Gramps's ribs.

His gaze followed hers. Etched against the sky on a high rise above them a motionless figure watched. The distance between them dwindled due to the clear Wyoming air. Cricket could clearly see the overall-clad figure astride a magnificent horse. Sunlight streamed on tossed golden hair. The man held his hat in one hand and the reins of his horse in the other.

"I'd say that's a real man," Gramps approved.

A snort from their middle-aged driver broke the spell. "Guess he is."

"Who is he?" Cricket asked, wondering why it mattered. Hadn't she sworn off men?

"The boss. Well, one of them. William and Martha Ames are partners with their son Loring." The driver warmed to his subject. "He ain't no dumb cowboy, either. He came home decorated from the service, headed off to college, then came home."

Cricket thought to herself, *A college-educated cowboy? Will wonders never cease.*

She said aloud, "Does Mr. Ames punch cows? Isn't that the right expression?"

"Right words but wrong job. Naw, the rest of us do that. Loring acts as a guide in the summer and does whatever needs doin' in winter." The driver swung the big car up in front of the log lodge with a definite flourish of pride. "Ain't nothin' around a ranch Loring Ames doesn't know and can't do." He sprang out, opened the doors, and began to unload luggage. "Matter of fact, there ain't much he don't know about this whole country."

"I can see we're in for some extraordinary times if the older Ameses are as interesting as their son," Gramps managed to mutter in Cricket's ear.

A sense of familiarity touched Cricket when William and Martha Ames descended the steps from the wide porch and greeted them, each automatically catching up pieces of luggage. When they shook hands with Gramps she realized what it was — all three had the same steady look, the same lack of self-consciousness. She marveled not at Gramps's ability to put the ranchers at ease but at their obvious lack of feeling a social difference between them and their guests. Nothing could have done more to make Cricket feel welcome — and anonymous —

than the look in Martha and William's clear eyes.

For three wonderful days Cricket wandered flower-strewn meadows within sight of the house, as ordered. She watched the ranch hands at work and wondered at their friendly but respectful manner toward her. Mostly she drank in enough Wyoming air to clear her heart, mind, brain, *and* lungs!

Gramps put his time to good use as well. He'd immediately taken a liking to young Loring Ames, who evidently seemed content just to work the ranch.

"How would you like to work for me?" Gramps asked one sunny afternoon, leaning against the corral.

Loring's bright blue eyes darkened and he coiled his lariat and hung it on his saddle. "No, thanks. I spent my time away. Four years in the service as a thanks for getting to be an American then four years at college because the folks had their hearts set on it. Now I'm home."

"I can offer money and prestige." The slightly begging tones of his own voice amused Charles. He couldn't ever remember having to ask a second time to get someone to work for him.

Loring straightened. Contempt faded before Charles's steady gaze. He pointed to the winding Snake River, the stands of un-touched timber, the snowcapped peaks. "I reckon God's already given me all the riches I need and prestige doesn't count."

Cricket rounded the barn in time to hear Loring's last words. God again! Yet she saw the same peace in this rugged man's face as she had seen in Mary Marshall's eyes.

Neither of the men looked toward her and she stole closer, intrigued with their conversation.

"Young man, someday you'll want to marry. When you do, you won't be so quick to turn down such an offer as I'm making."

Strong laughter sang in the air. Loring's face lit up. "Mr. Lee, the kind of girl or woman I marry won't be some flirty, pampered darling who expects me to leave everything I love and become as useless as she probably is."

Cricket shivered in spite of the warm air. How he despised the kind of girl he'd described — and the description fit her like a size seven glove! Intrigued but disappointed, one curious thought surfaced: Her vow to forget men had been made *before* she met one Loring Ames.

"So what kind of girl *would* you marry?"

"Please, God, one just like my mother." The brown hands finished their task and stilled. A poignant light filled the blue eyes. "Since the war a lot of girls and women have gone wild with the new freedom they claim is now theirs. It's a lot of nonsense. God never created people to be parasites. Neither did he create man and woman to struggle for supremacy as some of my married friends are now doing. Fifty years ago men and women worked together plowing and planting. So did Dad and Mom. When God sends along the person I'm supposed to marry, she'll be three things. First, as dedicated to Him and His Son the Lord Jesus Christ as I am. Otherwise, neither of us could be happy. Next, she'll be a real pard, someone I can trust and who'll ride the trails and laugh and enjoy life with me. Third, she will be the one I love with all my heart and soul and who feels the same about me."

"Isn't that a pretty tall order, as you boys say out here?" A bit of Gramps's cynicism spilled out.

"Not at all." Loring lounged against the corral fence and smiled. "Life here isn't easy. But by putting God first, then each other, and ourselves last, don't you think that will make a team that can pull in harness even when things get tough?"

Cheeks burning, Cricket slipped away,

glad not to be caught or seen. Of all the astonishing things she'd encountered in her few days in Wyoming, this topped the list. Who would expect to find such an idealist in the wilds of Tillicum Ranch?

Yet looking at it from his viewpoint, and obviously he had given it a great deal of thought, were his requirements really so stiff? Cricket paraphrased under her breath, "A strong Christian. A good sport. Someone who loves him."

She suddenly envisioned Cliffton Marshall's face after he had kissed her in that demanding way. Protest rose in her heart. Why couldn't Cliff have been more like this educated rancher with his platform for living? Both had served overseas, yet how differently they had reacted.

Would she like having God first if she ever relented and trusted another man enough to promise herself in marriage? What would marriage to Loring Ames be like?

"Who cares?" she demanded fiercely. "Imagine Charity Endicott meeting his qualifications even if living out here and being a rancher's wife weren't impossible." The feeling of uselessness that had intermittently troubled her since the accident she witnessed at seventeen returned stronger than ever. Cricket Lee *could* become something more than the flirty, pampered darling Loring disdained, couldn't she?

Not without hurting Gramps. Cricket beat at the bars of her cage, passionately wishing she could fly free and hating herself and Loring for reminding her how little she counted in things that really mattered.

Her near-black eyes glistened and she impatiently tossed her short curls that shone blue-black in the sun. *Silly to care what this Wild West rancher thinks,* she taunted herself. *Find something to do and you'll forget it. Anyway, he has no idea how wealthy you are.* She hugged her secret close without analyzing why.

The next afternoon her tenuous security snapped. A new guest arrived at Tillicum Ranch for an indefinite stay.

Dapper and dark haired, his dark eyes triumphant, Barney Delevan lounged on the wide front porch and sprang to his feet when Cricket returned from a rare ride with Loring Ames.

6

The sight of Barney Delevan nonchalantly coming toward her doused Cricket's high spirits like ice water. For two hours Loring had checked out her riding ability before grudgingly agreeing she could be trusted out of sight of the ranch — *if* she always rode Buckskin.

"Why do you call him Buckskin?" She patted the dark mane and tail that highlighted her mount's smooth golden hide.

"Because he is."

Cricket's laughter pealed across the level stretch of countryside between clustered evergreens.

Loring's eyes crinkled in response. "We're pretty direct out here. We call things what they are." He pointed to a slowly moving band of horses ahead of them. "There's Bay and Sorrel and Pinto and Black and —"

"Stop," she pleaded and held up a gauntlet-sheathed hand. Her well-cut riding habit, tailored by a master of the trade, blended with the soft browns of the landscape. "What if you get more than one buckskin or bay or whatever?"

He raised an eyebrow. "Simple." Again he pointed. "There are Sorrel Two and Bay Three and Pinto Two." The designated horses raised their heads. "Your horse was our first buckskin so he doesn't get a number." He didn't add that Buckskin had been his pet, raised from a colt and hand-broken. Or that after noting the girl's superb horsemanship he determined she'd have the best and safest. She wouldn't be held to the home pastures for long and if she did get caught out somewhere Buckskin had the wisdom to bring her home.

"If you're ever in trouble just let the reins lay loose and trust in God and your horse," he advised.

Cricket had already fallen in love with the high-spirited horse. When she went home she'd buy him and have him shipped to Long Island, a reminder of her Wyoming stay. Why did a faint dissatisfaction gnaw at her at the thought of going back? The serrated edges of the Grand Tetons reared thousands of feet above her into cloudless sky blue enough to swim in — as blue as Loring's eyes. At other times they balanced heaping whipped cream clouds that blended in

with the snowy caps.

I will lift up mine eyes unto the hills . . . she couldn't remember the rest. Shy of asking her companion, she determined to see if Gramps knew. Somehow it seemed important to find out.

"Loring, how could you leave this peace and go fight?" She bit her tongue when his face closed against her; yet when he replied she felt glad she'd asked.

"That's why. The hatred and anger I experienced toward those who would destroy the world for their own greed and desire for power wouldn't let me stay home." He stared at the horizon but Cricket shivered at the look in his eyes.

"I was so young then, I never really knew what it could be like but I felt the same way," she confessed, and twisted her fingers in her reins. "I remember Gramps's face when we got word of some of the battles. . . ." Her voice faded.

"Jutland, Flanders, the Somme, the Marne, Argonne Forest. A hundred others, each claiming lives in a senseless slaughter that had to be fought so America and the world could live free from fear."

Again Cricket shivered. "Will there ever be a world without fear? Not just of war, but of a thousand other things?"

Some of the bleakness left her companion's face. He straightened in the saddle. Quiet joy erased the look that had cut Cricket to the heart. "One day the Lord Jesus will return. When He does, the world as we know it will end. Those who know and love Him will spend eternity in His Presence in a place He has described as so wonderful that even the heart of man has never been able to conceive of such beauty."

Cricket licked dry lips. Her heart pounded. "How do you know this?"

"The Bible tells me, and anyone who will read it." He threw back his head and looked up at the tall mountains. "I also know it because I've proved Jesus is trustworthy. He's the only person who will never let me down in any way, although I may let Him down."

"How can you be so sure?" Cricket leaned forward. "If this is true, why don't more people know about it and have the peace your family has?"

"It's available to everyone who wants to know badly enough to search. The Bible promises that when we seek Him *with all our hearts* we shall find Him." An unexplainable look touched his eyes and his steady gaze never left her face. "Miss Lee, that search is the greatest and most rewarding thing on earth. Think of it, having Jesus as your best

Friend, knowing no matter what happens He's with you."

Swayed by his earnestness she whispered, "Even in battle."

"Yes." Humility shadowed Loring Ames's face. "*Especially* in battle. I personally believe few of those who saw action in the war came home the same person."

"But some went the other way," she protested.

"Yes. Those who don't know the Lord became callous and hard. Those who took Him in their hearts or accepted Him in the trenches were upheld by their faith. I saw them meet death gladly, assured of a better life ahead."

His quiet voice brought tears to her throat. Gramps had been right that first day when he spontaneously recognized the worth of this heroic, educated westerner.

Before she could respond, Loring smiled and her cold shivers vanished. "May I tell you more sometime? I'm afraid we have to get back to Tillicum if we don't want to miss the boys' impromptu show they've planned for you and Charles." At her inquiring look he laughed. "He asked us to call him that and Dad and Mom have been Bill and Martha since you arrived."

"I know." She hesitated then capitulated

to western informality. "No reason why you shouldn't call me Cricket."

"Crickets are mighty cheerful creatures to have around," he told her solemnly. He turned his horse toward home. She followed, wondering about the twinkle in his eyes and inwardly howling at being classified as a cheerful creature.

They dismounted at the corral. Loring promised to show her how to care for Buckskin another day if she wished but reminded her the boys' patience wore thin. If she wanted to freshen up, she'd better hustle.

Cricket hummed a snatch of popular song and hustled toward the log lodge. Upon looking up she plummeted from mountain high to valley deep in a few seconds.

"What are you doing here?" She glared at Barney Delevan the way she would a rattlesnake that suddenly crossed her path.

"Came to see you, of course." He smoothed his mustache in the invincible male gesture she particularly hated.

"How did you find me?" Surely Mary wouldn't give her away.

"Just happened to notice a letter addressed to Cricket Lee waiting to be posted when I visited my dear sister," Barney said easily. "I said to myself, 'She's bound to need someone of her own kind out there in

Wyoming with a bunch of stupid sodbusters too dumb to appreciate her.' So here I am."

"By what stretch of imagination did you dare think you're my kind, Mr. Delevan?" Every ounce of proud Endicott blood rushed to her rescue and she swept up the steps intending to brush him aside the way she would a persistent mosquito. "Furthermore, I am much more appreciated here than I ever was on Long Island." The high respect given by every hand on Tillicum Ranch rose to heighten her anger.

"Hold on, Miss Endicott." He grabbed her arm and halted her in mid-stride but kept his voice low. "How would you like to have your new acquaintances know who you really are and that you'd have married a divorced man if he hadn't died?"

She balanced herself on a railing. "Just what do you want? Money?"

He raised an eyebrow. "Not at all. I happen to be flush just now after a few days at the track."

"Then why did you come here?" she demanded again.

"I suppose you could call it admiration?"

Cricket wrenched her arm free and slammed through the front door and upstairs to her room. A few minutes later Gramps stormed in.

"Did you invite that young pup here?" His eyes blazed.

"I'm not insane and don't shout at me," she blazed back, shaking with anger and frustration and the bloodthirsty wish a certain Barney Delevan had perished in the war.

"Sorry." Gramps calmed down and awkwardly patted her heaving shoulder. "He waltzed in here like he owned Tillicum, called Martha 'my good woman,' and demanded an immediate meal. Bill told him he'd eat when the rest of us ate, that this wasn't a boardinghouse but a family ranch with guests and if he didn't like it, Bill would personally drive him back to the train station." A glimmer of amusement crossed Gramps's face.

"Good for him. Of all the insufferable persons, following us out here."

"Obviously he saw you. What did he say? What does he want?"

"I'm not sure," Cricket confessed. She grabbed an expensive brush from the dresser and pulled it through her tossed curls until a snarl brought tears to her eyes. She repeated what Barney had said.

"The way I see it, he's out to take any opportunity that might work to his advantage," Gramps said shrewdly. His eyes snapped.

"Well, the worst he can do is tell the Ameses who we are. So what? They're too big to judge people until they hear both sides."

"Why did he have to come and ruin everything just when —" Cricket stopped. Just when what? When she had begun to feel there were a few men left on earth with true, high ideals and purposes? She blushed at the thought and then paled. No, it went far deeper. Loring's expression when he courteously asked if he could tell her more of his faith sometime had welded with her own inner emptiness. What would the advent of Barney Delevan do to the chances of riding alone again with Loring?

It didn't take long for her to find out. Without lying, and by omitting the fact he'd only known Charles and Cricket for a short time, he managed to convey a solid background of friendship. Gramps wanted to tell the Ameses straight out what Delevan was doing. Cricket restrained him, unwilling to see the scornful look directed at her that she'd seen from Loring when discussing postwar attitudes and morals. Neither did she want him to know how totally useless she really was.

For his silence, Barney Delevan extracted a price: Cricket's company. He never attempted to touch her; he just made sure to be at her side when the time came to walk, ride, or eat, giving the impression of closeness that didn't exist.

Gramps continued to rage. Cricket also raged, but in the privacy of her room. Loring reverted back to calling her Miss Lee and if he held any special memories of that one sunny day before the snake entered his Wyoming Eden no one knew.

One morning Barney requested transportation into Jackson to send a telegram. Several days later, as a result of that message, Barney's entourage arrived — a group of wastrels as lazy as himself. They cluttered the ranch, hampered the work, and drove everyone to distraction. Bill Ames swore that if he didn't need the money so badly he'd fire the whole lot of them clean out of Wyoming.

Cricket landed square in the middle. While her loyalties lay with the Ameses, she still feared their opinion of her should Barney carry out his threats to expose her true identity. Wouldn't they feel she was no better than the crowd who harassed them?

Little by little Barney drew her into that crowd, at first reluctantly, then from sheer boredom. Loring no longer had time for her. The sensitive girl wondered if she'd already been tried and convicted in his mind. The thought brought rich, red blood to her cheeks. So be it. Let him think what he liked. What right had he to judge her? So long as Barney didn't go beyond the bounds she had set, why not ride and walk with him?

Barney at times even proved an amusing companion; at last she caught glimpses of the big brother Mary had adored. But just when she did find good in him, Barney inevitably did something to remind her how cynical he'd become. He never discussed his part in the war. Once she asked and he changed the subject, but not before his ghastly face showed something of the same turmoil she had glimpsed in Loring.

Although Gramps worried about her close association with Barney, to all his protestations she merely replied, "He isn't so terrible after all. With Mary as a sister, he can't be all bad. Maybe he just needs a nice girl to straighten him out."

"God forbid!" Gramps threw up his hands and bolted.

A few days later Cricket swung easily into the saddle and took up Buckskin's reins. "Bye, Gramps. See you in three days." Buckskin took off toward the mountains well in advance of the party, led by Loring, that would sleep out, cook over a fire, and enjoy what Barney called roughing it.

Cricket had been shocked at how eagerly he anticipated the trip. She hadn't marked him as the outdoors type. Yet anyone who had been at the front must be used to that kind of living.

Although Gramps had gone on an overnighter, he preferred the feather beds and home cooking Martha Ames offered. The smell of fresh cinnamon rolls lured him to the kitchen in spite of an enormous breakfast at sunup. Let Cricket ride off. He'd have a roll. She couldn't get in trouble with Loring guiding the party.

Never had Cricket felt more alive than on that three-day trip. Sizzling steaks, campfire-roasted potatoes, dutch oven biscuits, and home-canned pickles enticed appetites swelled by fresh air and plenty of exercise. Barney had held up well and Cricket admitted a certain fondness for him and the others who complained but said they wouldn't have missed the outing for anything.

On the last night, stuffed and tired, the Tillicum Ranch guests lounged around the fire. Loring headed to the icy stream a little way from camp to get fresh drinking water. Never failing, the crystal clear water chilled teeth and quenched thirst better than all the fruit juice or coffee in the world.

Cricket restlessly shifted position on the needle-covered ground and finally decided to take a walk before absolute blackness, such as Long Island never knew, set in. Barney had vanished for once and Cricket rejoiced in her freedom. With a crowd always around she had no time to think. She approached a small stand of trees near the stream and out of sight of camp. A rustle stopped her, head up, ears sharp. "Loring?"

Harsh laughter answered her and Barney Delevan stepped out from the trees, bottle in hand. "Were you planning on meeting him here? A *common* cowboy?"

"Don't be absurd, and what are you doing with that bottle?" Cricket's involuntary leap of fear subsided. "You know the Ameses don't allow drinking."

"So?" He had never been more insolent and she realized now how long he'd been gone from the campfire.

"So get rid of it." She held out her hand. "Or I will."

"Think again, Miss Cricket Lee." He strode toward her and his eyes glittered in the dusk. "We'll just have a little drink and talk about our future." He stumbled over a half-hidden tree root, lurched to catch his balance, and the bottle arced, dumping its contents on Cricket and falling empty to the ground.

"Now see what you've done!" The stench of whiskey made her physically ill and brought back memories too painful to bear. She tried to brush it off and only succeeded in saturating her hands.

In a lightning move Barney leaped up, pinned both of her arms at her sides, and laughed. His breath betrayed how much he'd already consumed. So did his loss of control. "Now what are you going to do?"

His triumphant laugh enraged her. How could she have thought him anything but base? "You drunken beast! Let me go." She managed to get an arm free and struck out, hard.

A curse answered her. "All I wanted was for us to have a drink together." He tried to hold her twisting body.

"I don't drink, I never have," Cricket cried. "Stop pawing me, Barney Delevan, or I'll scream so loud Long Island will hear me." She fought again.

His hands slowly dropped. A mocking smile draped itself over his face. "And just who are you going to convince you don't drink when you smell like this?"

"That's your fault," she furiously told him and turned to flee while she had the chance.

"What's the idea?" Compared with Loring Ames's tone of voice the freezing river was warm enough to swim in. "I thought you knew we don't permit drinking. *Ever.*"

"Sorry." Barney brushed by and disappeared down the trail to camp.

"Miss Lee, I suggest you follow your friend back to camp. Another incident like this and you'll be asked to leave in spite of my regard for your grandfather."

Anger at Barney and her own stupidity in trusting him turned white hot at being unjustly accused. "I haven't been drinking. I *never* drink. And Barney Delevan is not my friend, no matter how it looks to anyone else. I told him to get rid of the bottle and he tripped and fell and the liquor went all over me. You can believe me or not. I don't care. As for leaving, you can't get rid of us until we want to go. We're paid up."

Loring's voice gave no indication whether he believed her. He said, "There are such things as refunds. A few times in the past we've been forced to take that method of ridding Tillicum Ranch of disturbing influences."

"You — you —" Sheer fury cut off her words.

"You aren't the first to come out here and

not fit in." He sounded tired, almost depressed. It checked her anger more than his coldness. "Maybe I just thought you were different from the herd who trail with low-down skunks like Delevan. That's my problem. Now if you'll get back to camp and into some decent clothes you'll feel a lot better."

She fled, more from the disappointment in Loring's eyes, barely visible in the heavy dusk, than from his accusations. Only after she explained to the others in a voice loud enough to reach Loring at the edge of the firelit circle that Barney had spilled liquor on her did she remember the young rancher's indictment of her and his hoping to find her different. She remained awake long after the silence of the Wyoming night surrounded her and only the stars kept vigil.

"Good morning, Miss Lee. May I help you mount?"

Cricket couldn't believe her ears. All through the sleepless night she had frozen and burned with embarrassment, hating the dawn when she must meet Barney and Loring.

A perverse streak prompted her to stare at him and reply, "No thank you. Barney will help me if I need it." She caught his involuntary start and the disillusionment in his face before he quickly masked his expression and moved on to another girl who readily accepted his offer.

"Not mad?" Whatever Barney's condition the night before, morning had brought reality. "Sorry if I got out of line."

Sensing Loring's covert look, Cricket tossed her head. "Just don't let it happen again."

They halted for lunch in a sheltered spot several miles from the ranch. In the rest period following it blond-haired Millie, the worst flirt in the bunch, made a final desperate bid for Loring's attention. Only a day or two remained before the group's departure.

"Mr. Ames, Loring, I wish I could stay out here forever."

Loring smiled the same smile Cricket had seen him use toward a cute but annoying kitten in the barn. "You'd never make it." His eyes swept the group and darkened when they rested on Cricket. "None of you would." He ignored the collective gasp and went on. "First, you all want to get married, or at least most of you. That's the way God created things. See?" He pointed across the quiet landscape. Two birds winged by. Two squirrels played tag in a nearby tree. Two marmots chattered then slipped into their ground holes.

"Two by two. But foxes don't mate with rabbits or wolves with deer."

Cricket made a little sound of protest and he turned to her. "Take Miss Lee, for instance, if she doesn't mind?"

"Not at all." She pretended to examine her boot.

"Suppose she met someone out here. He would have little to offer her — a simple home, hard work, devotion. On the other hand, what could she offer him?" He abruptly stood and shattered the disbelieving stillness. "Such a big subject. We could talk of the ability to live in a mountain cabin away from friends, family, and conveniences, listening to wolves howl, wondering if the food would hold out until spring. Could any of you sing, the way my mother did, even when she buried two children who died during winters so hard a doctor couldn't get through? I think not."

Cricket couldn't help the rush of emotion that threatened her. "I doubt any of us will ever be required to put it to the test, Mr. Ames."

"I pray you won't. Lives depend on the ability to adapt."

"Isn't he too divine for words?" Millie giggled when Loring busied himself with the horses. No one replied. Even Barney looked abashed. Cricket carried food for thought and a renewed sense of worthlessness all the way back to the ranch.

That night when Barney and his hangers-on limped off to nurse sore muscles, rejoicing over the fiesta the Ameses announced for a grand finale to their visit, Cricket stole to her grandfather's room. Her fingers felt sweaty and she found it hard to breathe.

"Gramps, have you thought about going home?"

Could that be disappointimment in his hooded eyes? "Why?"

"I just wondered if we could stay on. I mean, after the summer is over." She twisted her hands into fists behind her back.

"That depends on you." Keen gray eyes looked squarely into turbulent dark ones.

"What do you mean?"

"Martha says they can't and don't keep fall and winter guests. I wondered if you'd like to stay and I asked her." His eyes twinkled. "She says if we're willing to be family members and work our way we can stay."

"Work our way!" Cricket's eyes opened wide. "What would we have to do?"

"Cook and sew and chop wood. The

hands look after the stock that doesn't stay on the range."

Cricket saw her half-formed dream begin to fade before her eyes. "But I can't do those things. Do the Ameses know? Why can't we just pay more and stay?"

"It's this way or leave, Cricket."

She walked to the window and stared out at the mountains she'd come to love. The verse that had haunted her became clear at last. *I will lift up mine eyes unto the hills from whence cometh my help.* How could she leave? Yet how could she stay subject to such conditions?

Loring Ames, freshly shaved and in clean clothes, laughed beneath the window.

"You'd never make it," he had told Millie. "None of you would." None including Cricket. The self-doubt she had carried for years was an insufferable burden. Maybe she wouldn't make it. Maybe Wyoming and Loring Ames and howling wolves and winter would defeat her, but not because she refused to fight.

Cricket turned toward Gramps, noting how much better he looked since they'd been at Tillicum Ranch. "Well, Gramps, looks like we're going to become ranchers. I hope you aren't so soft from business and Long Island living that you can't milk cows and muck out the stables. The Ameses will be mighty disappointed if you can't do your share."

She looked toward Heaven with an imploring glance then back out the window to the Tetons. "Now if I can only get rid of Barney Delevan."

7

"If you don't tie a can to that young upstart, I will. Mary warned us, remember?"

Cricket sighed. "Only too well." But her mind turned to other things. "Gramps, don't tell the others we'll be working for our keep. Please?"

Charles Lee Endicott raised an inquiring eyebrow. "Too proud to let them know you're going to learn something new?"

Cricket shook her shining head. "No. They'd just make fun and not understand. By the way, just how did you happen to be talking with Martha?" She turned accusing eyes on her grandfather. "Or was this all Mr. Ames's brilliant idea? You two are thicker than the proverbial thieves and have been ever since we arrived."

Wounded innocence sprang to Charles's face and Cricket turned her back on him to remove her boots. Was that a chuckle?

"Oh, no. Big Bill said it was entirely up to Martha. He would enjoy having us around

121

but the burden would fall on her."

"I didn't mean *that* Mr. Ames. I meant his son, Loring." This time Gramps cackled out loud, bringing the girl facing him in a hurry, resentment in her eyes.

"On the contrary. He wanted no part of it. Said why should his mom spend a lot of time teaching some girl something just because she had a whim to stay a few extra days? He thought it was pointless. Thought you'd tire of it before you learned anything anyway. When Martha said she'd give you a try, he stalked out looking like the young god he resembles when he's disgusted!"

Tears of fury filled the eyes dark as a duckling's breast. "I'll show him! I'll stay here, right in his home, until I can bake and cook and. . . ."

"I believe you. You don't have to convince me." If Cricket hadn't been so upset she would have seen the beginning of a satisfied smile creep over the cynical, worldwise face. As it was, he just patted her shoulder. "Honey, I think we're in for a real spell of unusual weather." His deliberate drawl made her laugh. As long as Gramps believed in her she would do her best to prove useful. Funny how he had changed. Look how he'd raved when she wanted to be a nurse so long ago. Now he acted eager for her to stay here

122

and learn from Martha Ames.

For a moment Gramps eyed her narrowly. He saw the determined Endicott chin but he also saw the beauty and strength of the first Cricket. With a little sigh he hoped this experiment would prove worthy. If only he had spent more time with her while she grew up maybe he wouldn't be so worried now. No use in worrying over what was past; the future had enough uncertainty.

"How would you like to go the whole way?"

"What do you mean, Gramps?"

"Well, as long as we're doing this little experiment, playing at being common people instead of the kings of the earth," he said sarcastically, "why not tuck away all the money we brought except the amount we'd have if we were really part of the Ames family? If an emergency came up, it would be there but in the meantime, we'd live just as they do."

Cricket didn't hesitate. Her wonderful eyes glowed with mischief. "Let's! I only need a gown for the fiesta, then — oh, you mean start right now?" Visions of frothy flounces died hard. The fiesta had provided an excuse for party clothes and Cricket loved new and pretty clothing.

She sighed. "I don't suppose the Ameses

will buy new outfits." What could she wear that she had? She wavered. It was too much, this was carrying things too far. And yet the curious look in her grandfather's face caused her to tilt her imperious chin even higher.

"That's right. They'd make do with what they have tucked away in the attic . . . the attic!" Excitement lit up her face. "I wonder if Martha would have something in the attic I could borrow."

"Trot down and ask her," he advised, quickly covering his pride. She evidently was going to fall in, go the whole way. In a few minutes she stuck her head in the door, key in hand triumphantly.

"She said she wouldn't tell. Whatever I find I can borrow for the fiesta!" The door banged behind her and Gramps sat in the big shabby chair waiting. She must have been gone almost an hour but when she came back her hands were full of garments, her cheeks scarlet as the silk draped over one arm.

"I can hardly wait for a rainy day. Gramps, you can't believe what's in that attic! There's even a spinning wheel. It's like stepping into history. I bet everything their grandmothers and great-grandmothers before them owned is stored in that attic. It's a treasure chest. You have to go with me one of these days and just look. But look what I found!"

Cricket pirouetted in front of the dresser mirror, gown held in front of her. It was a Spanish senorita's gown made of tiers and tiers of glorious crimson silk ruffles. Each ruffle was edged in black Spanish lace. To complete the ensemble was a black lace mantilla with a large red rose. With Cricket's dark beauty there was no reason why she shouldn't make a convincing senorita. Never had Gramps seen her more beautiful, even in the coming-out white dress with crystal fringe she had worn. The difference was in the expression. That debutante had been proud, even haughty. This senorita was excited, interested, and vitally alive to the possibilities that lay ahead.

Gramps's heart bounded. He had had some serious misgivings about this new venture in spite of feeling it would be good for the girl to know "how the other half lived," as he wryly put it. She had never known the joy of work he had been granted; it was only fair, even though the lessons might be hard.

"You look beautiful." Simple words, but the shining-eyed vision caught the significance of them. More than once he had told her she was the "spittin' image" of her grandmother. What it must mean to be here with her in Wyoming where he and her grandmother had spent their honeymoon so long ago! If she had qualms about the future, they were lost in the feeling she caught from him. He wanted to stay; he loved it here. In the days since they had come he had lost that tired, worn look. It was up to her to see he stayed that way. If he could rest and be content on this crude ranch, she would work her fingers to the bone. She laughed a bit at the cliché. First those fingers would have to be trained to work, let alone get near the bone!

When Loring Ames had stood by the corral gate stroking Ring his quiet fingers didn't reflect the inner turmoil he felt. Mom had told him of Gramps's proposition and he had protested but Mom had been firm.

"If the girl really wants to learn, I'll teach her." Loring had argued but to no avail. Now he didn't even notice the long line of cottonwoods swaying in the breeze against the blue sky he loved so well. They would be stuck with her, with a girl who upset him more than he'd admit. He deliberately shut his mind to the good things he knew of her, the evidentiy sincere enjoyment of his country, the love of the outdoors, the appreciation of his own Buckskin although she didn't know the horse was his, the look in her eyes when she seemed mentally to draw apart from the others and watch the clouds or a hawk sailing high. Instead he conjured up her angry face, her contemptuous questions, her haughty reply when she had turned down his help for Barney's that morning.

"I can hardly wait," he told himself bitterly. "As soon as the others leave we'll be one not so happy family. . . ."

The next morning the others could hardly wait to get into town and buy something for the fiesta. They couldn't believe Cricket wasn't going.

"How come?" Barney eyed her suspiciously. She had been careful not to act differently toward him at breakfast. She had a feeling that if she did he would suspect she had meant what she said about not going home with them that night. In a bold stroke she planned to go with them to the station, even board the train just as if she were going, then when it was too late for them to protest, slip off the train and stay. Her face burned at the thought of her deception but she had decided it was the only way. If they knew, especially Barney, they would protest, ruin the fiesta, and some might even insist on staying.

So now she lifted innocent eyes to his question. "I already have a dress for the fiesta. Gramps and I are taking a short ride this morning and then we'll come back and rest until lunch so we'll be fresh for the rodeo part." The man's suspicions were allayed. He knew Loring Ames was going into town. Reluctantly he went with the others. There was nothing in his wardrobe that would make him shine above the others. He had to get a costume that would dazzle Cricket and show her how much more desirable he was than anyone else. It was his nature to be the best, the most flattered, the most looked up to. He already had in mind what he wanted, if the hick town could provide it.

Barney Delevan had underestimated the town of Jackson. It was used to wealthy people, even millionaires. To that end the stores were well supplied with all the regalia for would-be cowboys, cowgirls, senoritas, and the like. The outrageously high prices for completely impractical costumes were offset by their glitter and glamour. To Delevan, Millie, and the others, price was no object, and by the time they returned at lunch with their purchases, they were in seventh heaven. Not a one among them felt he or she hadn't collected the ultimate outfit. They burst upon Cricket with ensembles of silk, satin, implanted jewels, sequins, and lace. Yet in her heart Cricket knew none was as lovely as the old-fashioned dress Mrs. Ames had so graciously loaned. The girls begged to see her costume but she only smiled mysteriously. Let them wait for it!

Lunch was a panorama; there was no other word for it. With Millie in a white satin cowgirl outfit with royal blue facings and sequins and Barney in purple and orange, the observant Tillicum Ranch cowhands beat a hasty retreat to the barn. Cricket could hear their loud "Haw haws" trail behind them and she smiled in sympathy. The staid ranchers had perhaps never seen such a brash display of color as pompously strutted in their lifetimes. Loring's face had a bitter twist. The money that had been spent on garments for that one day would have provided a living for him and his family for many months. He caught Gramps's eye.

"Peacocks," the old man muttered to Loring. "Just peacocks." Loring laughed. He had begun to respect and become fond of the crusty old millionaire. If only his granddaughter were more like him! But Loring's eyes opened wide when she came to the table, a little late. She wore dark brown riding pants, a simple yellow long-sleeved blouse, dark brown vest, boots, and a comfortable sombrero.

"Cricket, where's your outfit?" There was a general outcry. It was unheard of that the girl who was their recognized leader in both style and daring should not dress up for the rodeo.

"I'm saving mine for the barbecue and square dance," she told them coolly. She had caught the look of approval in Loring's eyes when she walked in. It made her furious that she had started a bit and that color filled her face. Anyway, she smugly reflected, he can see I'm not all fluff.

"It's going to be quite a square dance," Barney told her meaningfully, motioning to his jacket pocket where there was a conspicuous bulge from his ever-present flask. Cricket's heart sank. Was this to be a repeat of the night before last?

But she had not reckoned on the keen glance of her host, Bill Ames, who was no one's fool. Just before they finished lunch he stood to his feet, kindly, silver haired, smiling, yet firm.

"Now, people, we want you to have a good time your last day with us. We've planned a pretty full schedule and I think you'll like it.

There is one thing though." His pleasant glance encompassed them all.

"I don't suppose any of you have liquor you are planning to use, but just in case I will say one thing. What you do on your own time is your own business. But today there's going to be a lot of noise, a lot of confusion. There will be excited horses and more excited people. One of the reasons some of the guest ranches quit having fiestas was because a few people tried to turn them into drunken brawls. The last one a neighbor had ended with a . . ." he started to say tenderfoot and substituted, ". . . an inexperienced person with guns who lost control and managed to shoot himself in the foot. It gave our simple pleasures a bad name. The same way with the square dances. What started out as innocent games ended in fights. So if any of you have liquor, I suggest you keep it put away."

"What a prude!" Barney hissed through his teeth to Cricket, but Gramps noted her relieved look. Had that young pup been annoying her? It was a new thought, one for Gramps to digest. He looked pretty spiffy himself in his riding clothes. Cricket was proud of him.

Cricket hadn't known how many people were within "neighbor" distance of the

131

Tillicum Ranch. Lunch was barely over when wagons, cars, carts, horses, and every type of conveyance imaginable started coming. By two o'clock there must have been over a hundred people gathered around for the fiesta. How could Martha take care of them all? Cricket soon had her first lesson in Wyoming hospitality. Each family brought something for the barbecue. The giant iceboxes were soon stuffed with every kind of salad and vegetable and the pantry shelves fairly groaned under the burden of cakes, pies, and cookies. Outside three men carefully tended the whole steer on the barbecue spit. Its mouthwatering smell assailed her nostrils every time she passed it. In spite of lunch, it made her hungry then. Could she ever wait until six that night?

The guests were in for a real treat. There was a large area on the Tillicum Ranch reserved for just such occasions. Rude seats had been set up, the cleared space ready, and even the most disinterested, jaded socialite couldn't help but lean forward in awe at the display of horsemanship! Trick riding. Rope work. Bulldogging. Calf-tying. Barrel racing. And always among the first and foremost was Loring Ames. He sat in his saddle as if he had been welded to it, yet moved as one with his horse. He was using his own horse today, Buckskin, that Cricket had learned to appreciate so much. In Loring's own buckskin outfit they made a picture of oneness, striking, yet never showing off. Cricket saw him time and again move to the front of the other horses competing, then allow them to close part of the gap before winning. He would not flaunt over the others his superior riding.

It was an afternoon to remember. The sun was warm and bright but not unpleasant, due to the high altitude. In spite of the early season, a faint tinge of powdered sugar snow had appeared on distant peaks that very morning, reminding all that summer was nearly over.

To Cricket the highlight of the entire event was a simple, kindly act. Loring had been presented a sheaf of wildflowers for his riding. It was expected of him to give them to his best girl. She held her breath, suddenly jealous of whatever rosy, healthy Wyoming ranch girl he would choose. As he scanned the crowd leisurely the girls in her group almost held their breath. Would he by chance choose one of them? Yes, he started their way! Straight toward them he came . . . who would it be? Then before Loring reached them he stopped Buckskin, dismounted, and laid the flowers in the arms of a small girl just below them, a little girl with her leg in a cast, the victim of a birth defect, but whose glorious smile radiated! In another moment Loring had caught her up, cast and all, remounted, and rode around the ring with little Belinda in his arms, applause ringing as people stood in tribute to the kind act of a man who cared.

8

Long trestle tables formed by boards over sawhorses supported the weight of a sumptuous buffet. What with all the excitement of the events of the afternoon, everyone was in high spirits. Neighbors laughed and called to each other. Small boys darted in and out of the crowd, trying to steal tempting morsels from the table before time to eat, more often than not receiving sharp raps on the knuckles with the big spoons their mothers would use to serve. Little girls aped their big sisters in the long party gowns or cowgirl outfits of every color imaginable.

Millie had outdone herself in her choice of a gown, having purchased a costly Mexican wedding dress. Snowy white and lacy, the folds of the white mantilla enhanced her beautiful blond hair and large blue eyes. She nodded complacently at herself in a mirror before going downstairs, deliberately late. But those same childish blue eyes hardened, and even took on a slightly green color, when she saw Cricket standing against a background of leaves. Some of the hands had placed boughs and colored leaves near the tables where the guests would be served. In spite of herself, Millie gasped. Was Cricket part Mexican? No, she knew she wasn't, but her own senorita outfit paled before the vision standing there.

The scarlet ruffles that cascaded to the shining black pumps, the high-dressed black hair with the black lace mantilla and red rose, but most of all the genuine eagerness in the midnight black eyes set Cricket apart from even the most gorgeous competitor. Controlling her envy, Millie pasted a smile on her face and slipped to Cricket's side. At least, she would stand near. Cricket's dramatic costume would serve as an effective foil for her white outfit and blond coloring. Trust Millie to take advantage of any opportunity.

She may be more beautiful, Millie thought to herself savagely, but she doesn't even try and flirt! I can hold my own with her! The thought erased the last trace of annoyance from the smooth pink and white face.

"My, but don't you look nice." Millie appealed to Loring Ames who had approached. With a long look under her lashes she fluttered on, "Doesn't she look just like the real thing, Mr. Ames?" It was a good thing Loring had caught sight of Cricket across the yard before coming face to face with the two girls, both beautiful yet so unlike each other.

"Yes, just like the real thing." Cricket couldn't detect if he was being sarcastic, but chose to bestow a radiant smile on him and a deep curtsy.

"Thank you kindly, sir," she said meeting his eyes challengingly even though she was laughing. She knew he recognized the dress and she was grateful for Loring not giving her away to Millie. "Thanks again." This time he caught the underlying tone in her voice. His blue eyes lit up with a mischievous grin.

"Think nothing of it. The ranch is proud to host such a beautiful senorita . . . *two* beautiful senoritas," he added, including Millie with another smile. She lapped it up and turned on her charm full force.

"You will take me to dinner, won't you, Mr. Ames? I've been wanting to ask you," she tucked her hand under his arm, lifted innocent eyes to him, and determinedly led him away, continuing her conversation in a tone too low for Cricket to hear. The proud dark beauty stood there for a moment enjoying Loring Ames's evident discomfort, smiling wickedly to herself. Served him right for stepping out of his usual role and trying to flatter! Yet her eyes lingered long on the dark-clad figure with the ruffled white shirt of the Mexican matador. His peculiar shade of golden hair gleamed in the light of the many lanterns hung for atmosphere.

"May I take you to dinner?" The elder Mr. Ames, with a likable grin, was bowing low.

"Why, yes, Mr. Ames." She accepted his arm then looked around anxiously.

"Martha has your grandfather with her." The older man caught her searching glance. He motioned to where Gramps in a high chef's hat and large apron was rather inexpertly helping his wife serve. Cricket choked back a laugh then couldn't help but tease, "Well, good for her! It's time he learned something useful!"

Her smile won Big Bill Ames over completely. There was good stuff in this young lady. If she would only learn from his wife, she could turn out to be quite a gal. How the society world in which Cricket moved would have howled at the thought! But strangely enough, although Cricket caught his look, she no longer resented it.

She felt comfortable with this big, weather-beaten man. Furtively she studied the worn features, the hard, calloused hands. Here was no man of leisure. Yet for some strange reason she felt closer to him than to any of her own crowd. She had a feeling that you could put your head on his shoulder and be comforted.

"Were you ever a shepherd?" Bill Ames's ringing shout of laughter suddenly attracted the attention of several around them.

He lowered his voice before answering confidentially, "Don't ever ask a cattleman *that,* Cricket!"

She quickly joined him in a laugh. She knew enough from history and local stories that cattle ranchers and sheep herders weren't always the best of neighbors. The question had just popped out because he reminded her of a kindly shepherd of the flock. He would also have made a good minister. It was another new thought to the girl, one to be considered later, taken out and dissected. There was no apparent reason for the comparison. Cricket's knowledge of churches was practically nonexistent. Except for serving as bridesmaid for her many friends, her attendance had been nil. Yet deep inside the thought persisted: If I knew a minister like that, in fact, if the world had many ministers like this man, wouldn't more people go to church?

The dinner was over and the musicians were tuning up for an old-fashioned square dance. Cricket marveled at the pure enjoyment on the faces of the guests. Not only did the neighboring ranch people look forward to it, her own set, including Millie, could hardly wait! Tomorrow they'll all be gone, she pondered. Cricket herself slipped a little way from the crowd, noting with interest the large stars.

Someone came up behind her and without turning she asked, "Are they really larger out here, or is it just that the air is cleaner?"

"Who cares?" The demanding hoarse voice brought her back from her study of the heavens and the beauty of the distant peaks against the dark-blue sky. Barney Delevan had succeeded in finding her at last. He had been outraged when she had gone to dinner with their host, but was slightly mollified it had been the elder Mr. Ames, and not his son. He had nursed his grudge during the excellent meal, watching for a chance to regain his usual position at Cricket's side. If he had considered her worthy of himself before, this night he had seen the girl as she really was. He had literally gasped at first sight

140

of her radiance when he came to dinner. Despite Mr. Ames's request, he had fortified himself with several drinks in his own room and now his veins were on fire. The sight of Cricket in that red dress fueled his determination that not another night would pass before she promised to marry him. For the first time in his life he was in love, for better or worse. Once having seen her so, he must selfishly reach out and pluck the flower before others fully realized how choice she was! Now the sight of her watching those stars, alone, brought about the exact situation he had hoped.

"Who cares about the stars? A few hours from now we'll be on our train headed home!" Before she could catch his intention he caught her close, fiercely holding her. She smelled the liquor on his breath. This time there was no Loring Ames to help her! Until that moment Cricket had been apt to overlook some of Barney's faults, excusing him because of his background. But with his repulsive breath hot in her face she knew with sudden clarity that never, never would she marry a drinker. First Cliff, now Barney . . . she couldn't take it, and to think how much worse he would be if she belonged to him! Something inside her shriveled at the idea. But in those lightning moments of realization she also gained strength from her heritage. If she struggled it would be no use. Barney's strength was superhuman when he was drinking, in spite of his dapper build.

As the man's arms closed even more closely around her, Cricket stood absolutely still, lifeless as a piece of cardboard. The unexpected lack of response startled Barney for a moment and he loosened his grip. Quick as a flash she had ducked away and was running back to the others with all her speed. The long dress hampered her, she could hear his heavy footsteps behind, even gaining on her, and then full force she ran into a large, immovable object!

"You!" She gasped, most of the breath knocked out of her against Loring Ames's ruffled white shirt front. She felt annoyance mingled with relief — did it always have to be *him?* But before she could say more he asked, "Am I intruding — again?"

Too furious with Barney, Loring, and the world at large to reply, Cricket uttered an inarticulate cry of rage mingled with hot tears and fled to the side door of the lodge, not slowing her pace until she reached the quiet sanctuary of her room. Throwing herself on her bed she wept tears of anger, disgust, and shame. Yet facing herself squarely, perhaps more openly than ever before, she had to admit she had asked for it. In her efforts to show Loring Ames how little he mattered in her scheme of things she had too easily accepted Barney back in her good graces. What else could she have expected? The thought brought on another torrent of tears, and it was a rather subdued young lady who washed her face, repaired her hairdo, and went back downstairs. She had thought of feigning a headache, but her curiosity was too much — she had to find out what happened to Barney!

Cricket arrived downstairs just as the front door was flung open. There stood an immaculate Loring Ames, half-supporting a totally drenched Barney Delevan by a grip on the smaller man's collar.

"Mr. Delevan fell into the horse watering trough," Loring explained easily. "I'm just helping him up to change for the dance." Without a word Cricket stepped aside, but the look of hate Delevan shot toward Loring made the girl shiver. It was a good thing Barney was leaving tonight. After they had gone she stood staring up the staircase until she was roused from her stupor by a cackle. She spun around to see Gramps doubled over in the kitchen doorway.

"What are you doing in there?" she accused, but he only laughed harder. Had she ever seen him so amused before? Cricket thought not.

"Martha sent me for more ice for the punch." It was all he could do to talk. "I thought it was only in the old cowboy and Indian tales that drunks were sobered up in horse troughs!" Cricket couldn't believe her ears.

"You mean it wasn't an accident?"

"Accident!" The old man bent double again. "Not so you'd notice it!" He went into a fine imitation, punctuating it with terse remarks.

"In there, you." *Splash.* "You were told to leave that stuff alone." *Splash.* "Of all the rotters, you're the worst I've come across." *Splash.* "Get in there, you!"

Cricket didn't know whether to whoop or cry. Dropping limply to the bottom stair she accused, "And just where were you all this time?" The gray eyes took on an aura of innocence but the drawl was deliberate.

"Oh, I just happened to be moseying in the vicinity. . . ."

"You enjoyed it, didn't you?"

"W-e-ll . . ." His shoulders shook. "I'll bet Barney Delevan will have a healthy respect for Wyoming ranchers from now on."

"Ranchers! Loring is a guide, isn't he?" Now it was the old man's turn to stare.

144

"Loring!? It was his father who soused Barney Delevan!"

"His *father?* I don't believe it. Not that kindly man!"

Gramps drew his forefinger across his heart. "Cross my heart and hope to die," he told her solemnly.

"B-b-but where was Loring all this time?"

Her grandfather refused to meet her eyes squarely, squirmed, then answered, "He was busy following a lady in red."

Cricket was speechless. Had Gramps witnessed the whole event? And had the elder Ames seen it all too? They must have. Her white skin showed telltale streaks of color as a hot blush rolled up from the white neck. Gramps saw the tears start and suddenly abandoned the teasing, putting his arm around her.

"I'm sorry, honey. We really weren't spying. Bill and I had walked out to look at the stars. You were so engrossed in them we didn't want to intrude, but when you asked your question, he started to answer, and before he could, you know the rest." Yes, she knew the rest. These two fine men had seen Barney, his crude actions, her flight into Loring, and finally . . .

"Come to think about it, it is funny!" Cricket's irrepressible sense of humor began to make the best of the whole thing. After all, why worry over the past? They would all be gone tomorrow! Now as she noticed a puddle of water on the floor by the front door she giggled almost hysterically.

"Did you ever see such a sight, such a drowned rat as that Barney Delevan?" She and Gramps on the bottom stair rocked back and forth.

"And the way Loring held him by the nape of the neck, making sure he didn't drip on Loring's own outfit!" They were almost beside themselves with laughter. Upstairs in the long bathtub where the haughty Barney Delevan lay, quite sober now, he heard the laughter and wondered. But in the bedroom where Loring Ames was laying out a clean outfit for his troublesome guest, he heard and understood. A small smile crept over his features, his heart felt a little lighter. No girl who cared anything at all for a man, and saw him as Cricket had seen Barney Delevan, could have laughed!

Perhaps things wouldn't be so bad after all. He quickly sobered. Why should he rejoice in the thought? As a child of God, dedicated to the service of Jesus Christ, a girl like Cricket Lee could only be admired, never coveted. A grim line formed between Loring's brows and before he went back to his duties as host, a quick and fervent prayer shot skyward — a prayer for help and protection against a far different danger than anything he'd faced overseas.

After the early disaster the rest of the evening settled into more fun than Cricket expected. Had those moments on the stairs with Gramps restored her balance? Or had the secret knowledge of staying on when the others left buoyed her spirits? By the time Barney reappeared all her dances were promised and he could only stand back helplessly and watch her have fun. He was glad when it was over and they had waved goodbye to the Ameses. Loring was taking some of them to the station and others would go with a hospitable neighbor who said it was no trouble at all to drop them off. Their luggage had been taken in and checked earlier that day; all they had to do was grab last-minute items.

At the station Millie's tears flowed freely. She begged Loring Ames prettily to be sure and come East and see her. Barney's lip curled in scorn. You would have thought Loring and Millie had been sweethearts the way she carried on! Yet the big oaf only smiled. Barney threw him another glance of hatred. Only too well did he remember this man's iron grip and the iron grip of the father who had punished him for transgressing the ranch hospitality. With a sigh of relief Delevan literally shook the dust of the place off forever and went to find Cricket. The warning signal had sounded several minutes ago and she was probably in her own compartment now.

I wonder if she will speak to me, he mused, then sure of his own conceit, he began thinking how he could frame an apology that would get him by and yet let her know it was her own fault for looking so beautiful in that starlight. But when he reached her compartment, only Millie was there.

"Where's Cricket?" The round blue eyes looked at him in wonder. Millie had always admired Barney Delevan. It was one of the reasons she disliked Cricket. Now she saw a golden opportunity.

"Why, she was here just a moment ago." Barney failed to notice the fingers behind her that held a note addressed to herself and now tossed it back to the small table behind her. The train was gathering momentum and the farewell cries grew more intense.

"Why don't you sit down and wait? She should be back in a minute or so. Maybe she went to check on her grandfather."

"Her grandfather? I don't remember

seeing him get on the train." Barney's eyes took on a suspicious look. "What are you hiding, Millie?"

"Why, nothing!" Her eyelashes fluttered. To make her performance more convincing, she opened the door to the aisle. "Cricket, are you there?" When she turned back into the room she looked about, apparently surprised, then pointed. "Look!" Barney snatched up the white envelope on the table. Ignoring the fact that it was not addressed to him, he ripped it open. He recognized Cricket's writing only too well.

Millie used all her powers to remain wide-eyed and innocent. Only moments ago she had heard Loring Ames's low-voiced comment to Cricket, "I'll wait for you in the station." Not for anything would she tell Barney Delevan what she had heard. While a flirtation with Ames might be enjoyable, the opportunity to have Barney to herself on the trip back East shone bright in the grasping girl's mind. Her own fortune was nearly gone, she needed someone with money to back her. Why not Barney Delevan? If he had been watching he would have noticed the tip of a pink tongue licking her lips with much the same satisfaction of a cat in the cream. But with unbelieving eyes he was absorbed in the note.

Dear Millie,

Will you please tell the crowd Gramps and I aren't going home just yet? He is doing so well out here he wants to stay into fall, or possibly longer. Of course I can't leave him.

I'll let you know when we'll be coming home. Have a good season.

Cricket

With a rude comment, Barney threw the note to the floor. "We've got to stop this train! We'll get her and bring her with us in spite of what she says. I bet they had it all planned, she and that grandfather and the Ameses!" Never had Millie seen him like this. For a moment it frightened her. Was even all his money worth this kind of temper? But her own selfishness soothed the new thought.

"Why, what's the matter?" Snatching up the note, although she suspected what it contained, she read it and gave a horrified gasp. Clutching the man's arm as if for support she lifted tear-filled eyes in much the same way she had looked at Loring Ames.

"Oh, Barney, what will we do?"

"I'm going to stop this train!" He took one

step toward the door but with a well-calculated lurch only half-caused by the swaying of the train around the corner Millie fell heavily against him.

Her perfume filled his nostrils as she said, "Maybe . . . maybe you should let her stay." Seeing his look she hastened to add, "Of course, you know best, Barney, but you know she will get tired of this place when the snow comes and. . . ." Her voice trailed off, and with another movement she was close to him, gazing intently in his eyes. The man hesitated, stirred by those eyes. Although Cricket had never known it, Millie was one of those he had carelessly sought, conquered, and then dropped in the past. Now the memory of the good times filled him, along with the feeling she could be right.

"If she stays out here . . ." he said, thinking aloud. "When the snow comes, as you say, she will hate it. Charity Endicott, pampered darling. Of course! But in the meantime, Millie," his eyes held an invitation. "In the meantime I will be rather lonely. . . ." Now was the supreme moment, the height of Millie's acting ability. If she could only carry it off, he would be hers. "I'll take care of you, Barney," she whispered.

His still fuzzy brain cleared. Millie spent money like water. There must be millions

151

behind her. Why not grab a little old opportunity now? With a quick move he caught her close and cursed to himself that she wasn't Cricket.

Millie's heart leaped; Loring Ames's memory receded. Deep inside she knew he never cared for her and that even if she had wanted to live up to his ridiculous expectations of womanhood it wouldn't have been worth the effort.

Miles clacked off no more rapidly than Millie's plans. Nothing holier than thou about Barney. Her eyes brightened and she snuggled closer. No reason not to let him know how much she liked him, not in this enlightened day. Yet a small sigh escaped her painted mouth. If only he could be just a little like Loring Ames.

Cricket's carefully planned escape went so well she could scarcely believe it. Along with the rest of the eastbound passengers, she boarded the train. Not the private car this time, for they had clamored for her company. When she had honestly protested that Gramps hated traveling alone — without bothering to mention Gramps remained at Tillicum Ranch — they overrode her.

While the others milled in the aisles and

152

shouted farewells to the annoyance of sleepy passengers she vanished. No one saw her stride rapidly through car after car, coming at last to the end one. If her timing was right . . . it was. She reached the door just as the steps were being swung away from the train.

"Wait. I must get off."

"Step lively, miss!" The porter's strong arm landed her safely on the ground. In another moment the train had begun to move, but without a backward glance Cricket melted into the shadows, her dark coat chosen especially for blending into the night. She wouldn't put it past Barney to leap off the train if he saw her. But from the corner of the building, hidden from sight, she watched as it sped off, gaining speed with every minute, and smiled.

"You made it." Loring Ames's companionable grin clinched the feeling of escape and freedom. It was so out of harmony with the way he usually spoke to her for a minute she didn't respond. Then with a gamin grin she held out her hand.

"No, kiddin'! Meet Cricket En— Lee, new kitchen helper!" He took her hand, gripping it strongly, yet without a trace of presumption, and looked at her intently.

"Come." He led her to the station wagon

that had held their laughing, merry crowd just a little while ago. Silently he held the door then slid into the driver's seat for the ride home.

9

Barney Delevan had gone but his maliciousness had not. A week after he left Tillicum Ranch a bundle of carefully selected newspapers arrived, filled with accounts of Charity Endicott, Cliff Marshall, the plane crash, and court hearing carefully circled in ink as black as Barney's intentions.

Cricket's heart sank when she saw the amazement on the Ames family's faces. But her heart warmed when Bill observed, "Good picture of Charity Endicott but she doesn't look much like our Cricket."

"Our middle names really are Lee," Gramps set them straight. Loring's lips tightened but for once his eyes didn't condemn, and Martha put in, "Landsakes! No wonder you wanted to get away from all those goings on." Her eyes crinkled at the corners.

The very first day Cricket and Charles started working their way on the ranch Cricket bluntly confessed, "I don't know

155

anything." Her frank admission touched Martha Ames. "You'll learn. Just don't try to do everything at once, and don't get discouraged. You needed more than one swimming or tennis lesson, didn't you? Cooking and cleaning are the same way. I think you'd better just watch today or I'll give you simple things. You can learn a lot by standing back and watching." Her kind heart and big smile did a lot for Cricket's self-esteem. After all, it wasn't *her* fault she was so ignorant, it was only her fault if she stayed that way!

So as Martha Ames bustled about doing her chores Cricket followed at her heels, asking a hundred questions. While they worked Martha told the girl how things would be.

"You noticed there was just the family at the table. That's how we operate. The men really prefer eating in the bunkhouse, and Cookie's a dandy! His menus are pretty much the same as mine so we buy in quantity. In a few weeks when the snow flies a lot of the men will drift off for the winter — we can't use them. We keep a skeleton crew then. But when spring comes and we get ready for our 'dudes' they'll be back." Her hands were busy with flour, making a great pile of dough turn from a sticky mass into a smooth pile ready for kneading. She saw Cricket's look of interest. "Want to try it?"

"Sure! Is this going to be bread?" Martha didn't have the heart to laugh at the girl but told her solemnly, "Oh, yes. I like to bake my own bread. I usually bake twice a week, we use a lot of bread here." By now Cricket's small strong hands were floured and deep into the dough. But it didn't go the way it should. When she pulled one way, the sticky mass slid the other.

"Oh," she wailed, trying to get it off her fingers which had suddenly become all thumbs, "what do I do now?"

"Use more flour and keep with it." Martha was wise enough not to take over for the girl. Eventually the dough was tamed, although Martha privately wondered if dough that had been subjected to Cricket's ministrations would ever make bread fit to eat. But later shaped and rising in great pans in a warm place, Cricket's pride in having helped knead it was all out of proportion to the slight task she had been given. Was this housekeeping, the chore she had dreaded? Well, part of it, she admitted. She liked the cooking, the preparing of vegetables ahead of time, setting of puddings, handling dishes. She couldn't say the same for the cleaning! Martha showed her how to sweep the floors and although Cricket did a fairly creditable job her arms were tired long before she finished the big ranchhouse.

The dusting wasn't so bad. With a can of furniture polish and a big rag she polished the old-fashioned furniture until it shone. Time sped by and all at once Martha called her.

"My land! It's almost twelve o'clock. We've got to get dinner on the table." She whisked the big pot of baked beans out of the oven, pushed in the pan of cornbread she had stirred up in between other jobs, and shoved a great bowl of salad greens toward Cricket, telling her to wash and tear them.

"Tear them?" Cricket was helpless again, but in a few moments after Martha had shown her what to do she was happily making the salad.

There was quite a difference in the shining-eyed girl who came to the table that day from the one the Ameses had known as their guest. She had a slight streak of flour across one cheek where she unconsciously rested her hand. She also had a burn on one thumb from getting in too much of a hurry with the oven when she took out the cornbread. Her hair was slightly mussed; in the last moments of getting dinner on the table she hadn't had time to primp.

There was genuine enjoyment and pride in her voice as she announced, "And I made the salad!" Bill Ames's eyes met those of his son Loring across the table. There was amusement along with the revealing of just how little Cricket had known. If there was admiration Loring hid it but did tell her how good the salad was.

"Well, *I* fed the chickens, gathered the eggs, and helped feed the horses!" Cricket had almost forgotten Gramps that morning. He looked foreign to her in the overalls his host produced when Gramps confessed he didn't have any. But he also looked contented and rested. The gray eyes that were usually so steely and keen to see through a crooked business opponent shone with sheer enjoyment. Cricket put aside the temptation to nurse her burned thumb and was glad for him. It ached in spite of the cold water treatment Martha had ordered. Yet wasn't it worth it to see Gramps like this? Cricket remembered how pallid he had looked when he was sick, the soft-soled shoes of the nurses coming and going, the gravity of the doctors' faces. What was a burned thumb in comparison to his brimming spirits?

As the days passed Cricket had her share

of successes, and a helping of disasters. In fact, her first cake was a complete disaster. Light, tall, beautifully frosted, her pride was evident when she carried it in intact before cutting. She wanted them to see her handiwork. There was a queer silence over the table as they sampled. She of course hadn't tasted it yet. When she did . . .

"Oh, no, it's *salty!*" The tears were very close. That beautiful cake, ruined by a simple mistake no ten year old would make!

"It's not your fault," Martha comforted. "I had to move the salt into the sugar basin because I broke one of my ceramic cannisters!" Finally Cricket joined in the laughter. Just one more thing or "all in a day's work" as Loring Ames would say.

If Cricket had thought there would be less to do after the guests left she was in for a big surprise. In addition to the daily chores there was canning. The girl from New York City had never considered such a thing. Food came in cans from the grocery store, and the cook went and selected what she wanted.

"Tin can food!" Martha snorted. "Not on my ranch, if I can help it!" Martha's pride and joy was a huge vegetable garden. Recreation for her was working in her garden, and when after many weary hours she and

Cricket stood before the finished product, Cricket had to agree. There were quarts and quarts of every vegetable imaginable — beets, tomatoes, carrots, beans, peas, corn — and even broccoli and cauliflower. Shelves and vegetable bins were full. There were great stone crocks of pickles curing in their own brine. There were jars of jams, jellies, and apple butter. There were great sacks of potatoes, sweet potatoes, apples, turnips, and parsnips. Not only would the food carry them through the winter, it would help serve the next season's guests.

"We're through," Martha announced. "The men even have their butchering done. The hams and bacon are finished. Now let it snow!" It didn't seem possible. The days and weeks had passed, now it was late October. They had expected snow sooner, yet although the peaks grew more and more laden with their white burdens daily the valley had been free. Cricket stretched tired muscles. In all her socialite days on Long Island she had never been so content.

Cricket had begun to grow in other ways as well. Now that she and Gramps had changed status from guest to family member, they were included in the Ames family worship at the end of every day. The first time she heard Bill Ames read from the well-worn Bible the words sounded foreign. As she began to really listen to the story of the lost son, she found herself intrigued. Why had no one ever told her the Bible had such stories? She thought it was filled with musty warnings by prophets long dead, if they ever had lived.

Loring's firm, unembarrassed prayer, which included a simple "And thank you for the presence in our home of Charles and Cricket," brought a mist to her eyes and made her wonder. The armed truce that had existed since the departure of Barney and his cohorts melted into uncertain friendship after that prayer.

"Cricket —" Gramps tapped at her open door one gorgeous October afternoon.

"Come in, Gramps. I'm just writing to Mary." Her dark eyes twinkled. "Your matchmaking seems to be right on schedule. Listen to this from her last letter.

" 'And Mr. Endicott's reporter friend David Barrington has been most kind. Little Barney latches onto him every time he comes. Cricket, David is a real Christian. I wonder if God led me to Long Island for a reason. . . .' "

"Best thing that could happen to her and Barney," Gramps said gruffly. "He'd be getting a mighty fine woman as well." He cleared his throat. "Anything about that rapscallion brother of hers?"

"Yes. He's furious that Millie deceived him into thinking she had money when she'd wasted almost everything she inherited. Imagine that! Barney Delevan, angry because someone deceived *him!*" She threw back her head and laughed joyously.

For once Gramps didn't join in. "Hope that tinhorn doesn't take it into his head to show up out here again."

Fear and apprehension brushed Cricket's high spirits and she giggled. "If he does, we'll get our boys to tie a tin can to him, as you once suggested."

"Minx." But Gramps grinned and tousled her hair.

"Mary also said the lawyers you privately put to work have unearthed a few more assets and since we signed over anything remaining of Cliff — Cliff's estate," her voice broke. For a moment she returned in spirit to Long Island and her unhappiness. She quickly recovered.

"Anyway, there's enough to let Mary and little Barney live comfortably on their own. Mary says when we go back she'll get a little place not too far away. She wants to keep in touch. I hope she does. She's worth a dozen of my society girlfriends put together."

"Glad you have the good sense to see it," Gramps told her bluntly. He added, "Have you thought about going home?"

"Home? To Long Island?" She stared at his earnest face and her good mood plunged. "Don't you like it here?"

"Of course. But although the work has been hard up to now, you've been kept busy. But soon the snows will come. Life at the ranch goes on, it's true, but there will be little opportunity to ride or hike. You have managed to fit in some of that. Will you be happy staying inside except when someone has the time to take you out?" Her mind was whirling. She had thought Gramps wanted to stay into winter, and as for herself . . . leave now, after all that work? Go back to New York, never to know the joy of opening those shining quarts of fruits and vegetables she had helped make? Never to have those ever-present Grand Tetons smiling at her? Never to see Loring . . . she shut down hard on that thought.

"It's your decision, of course," her voice was colorless. Yet Gramps was wise enough to read her face.

"Think about it," he advised. "You can decide later."

Gramps's words haunted her the rest of the day, so much so that when they had all gathered around the fireplace that evening she spoke what she was thinking. She loved that great smoky fireplace with its mighty, snapping fires. Great sections of logs — birch, alder, she could almost tell the kind burning by the different odor — were split to size and threw out immeasurable heat.

"Gramps wants to know if we should go home."

"Home!" Three voices spoke in unison, three minds began clicking. Martha dropped her knitting into her lap with a little sound of dismay. Working day in and day out with this girl she had grown to love her. A true daughter could never have held a more special place within her heart. Home? A lump of misery began to form inside. Yet hadn't she always known it was only an experiment?

Home! Big Bill Ames's hands that had been skillfully carving a tiny figure stilled. He too had learned to love Cricket and both he and Martha admired Charles Endicott. Not for his millions, or his brilliance, but because he was a wonderful person.

Home! Loring's mouth twisted bitterly. So it had come. He had known it would, yet it was so unexpected. Of the three, he was the one who voiced the question in all their minds.

"Do you want to go?"

Gramps answered before Cricket could. "When we made arrangements it was to be for fall and into winter. Perhaps we've imposed on you long enough. Then, too, I'm not sure Cricket would like winter out here. . . ." His voice drifted away with a curl of smoke that had escaped from the fireplace upward into nothingness.

"Do *you* want to go?" This time Loring's voice spoke to the girl.

Throwing caution to the wind she blurted out, "No!" A glad light came into the eyes of those facing her, but she went on, "Maybe you don't want us anymore. We can't outstay our welcome. I've learned my lessons. That's what the bargain was. We've moved right into your family and. . . ."

"Not want you?" Martha's voice was incredulous. "You can't know what you and Charles have meant to us all!" She began to enumerate on her fingers. "The work. The opportunity to just have you with us. The laughter and fun. Now you are going away just when we have time to really visit? Or is your grandfather right, would you be bored?" Her question sounded light, almost trivial, yet Cricket could sense the underlying trust Martha had that it would be answered honestly. For a moment she hesitated, then smiled.

"I don't think so, but why don't you tell me about Wyoming winters? What happens, what do you do? I know what winter would be like in New York," she drew a quick breath, closing her eyes for a moment, visualizing the long, wet, lighted pavements, the plays and concerts, the never-ending charity benefits. Was she ready to go back to them so soon, even though she loved the thrills, the excitement? But Bill Ames's deep voice recalled her to the present.

"You realize of course that the housework goes on, the stock has to be cared for." She nodded and Gramps noted with approval her eagerness to hear. If it had only been himself he could have stayed here with these good people forever. Let someone else run the business. But he had to think of Cricket. If only . . .

"There are days when it snows, when we're kept inside. Some days we spend indoors except for necessary duties." His keen eyes glistened. "But those are days to treasure, child. All the things we don't have time for during the rest of the year are suddenly available! Time to chat, or just sit and look into the fire. Time to think. Time to read." His eyes turned longingly toward a great stack of magazines in the capacious bookcase next to his big chair.

"You mean read for information?"

"That, too, but mainly just for enjoyment!" Martha's eyes began sparkling in anticipation. "Remember when you were dusting and you asked about all the books? Many of them are old favorites of mine. Every winter I devour as many as I can; it is like getting back to old friends." Loring eyed Cricket narrowly. Would she understand? He sensed Cricket probably hadn't done much pleasure reading since she was a child. She probably dipped into the best sellers, a few magazines, and let it go at that. But he was wrong. Her face lit up.

"Oh, Martha! That's wonderful! When have I ever had the time to read the way I want to?" She cast a glance at the laden shelves with much the same look Martha had given them. "Every time I've dusted in here I've looked at those rows and rows. I'd be happy to stay here all winter just to get my hands on them."

"Good girl!" Bill Ames approved. "But we had other plans for you this winter too." He looked affectionately at Gramps. "Ever since you came, Charles, I've been wanting to just have time to sit down and talk world affairs, politics, history. Loring's always too busy outdoors and Martha just skims the surface. I knew we could have some good old visits when the snow is piled high." Gramps cackled.

"I also saw a chess board. I'll bet I can beat you at that!" But impulsively Cricket turned to Loring, who had remained silent for the most part, carefully evaluating each expression on her face. She sensed that while they had become friends in the time she had stayed in his home she had not yet won his complete approval.

"Do you want us to stay?" Her direct question startled him, yet it shouldn't have. If he had learned anything about this girl from another world it was that she was completely honest, even at times to the point of painfulness. Now he could be no less direct.

"I'd very much like you to stay. Besides what Mom and Dad have told you, I can offer sleigh and sled rides and sometimes horseback rides if weather permits, even a neighborhood get-together once in awhile. Cricket, Charles, we want you to stay. You can be here at Christmastime," he waxed eloquent. "We bring in a lot of the outdoors, decorate, and on Christmas Eve we have an open house. You'll be surprised how many people make it, no matter how bad the weather. On Christmas Day everyone who is left on the ranch worships and eats together; we make small gifts for one another, nothing expensive, just a lot of fun. It's a wonderful time of year."

He fell silent, remembering Christmases of the past. Through Cricket's mind flashed memories of her own holidays. They were so different from this simple way of life. Usually she and Gramps exchanged costly gifts on Christmas Eve, but on Christmas Day it was a round of parties, stretching into the evening and the annual Christmas ball at the country club. Suddenly those memories seemmed a bit tarnished and unsatisfying. To spend Christmas out here, with those mountains in the distance!

"Gramps?" Her wistful voice and pleading eyes told him what he needed to know and what he had hoped to say.

Clearing his throat, he stated, "We'll stay." But it was irrepressible Martha Ames who had the last word.

"Well, hooray! Don't know why you ever thought you might not!" They were committed: They would spend the winter on a lonely mountain ranch, while back in New York City their former friends and business associates would wonder if the pair had suddenly taken leave of their senses.

Loring waylaid Cricket when she started

up to her room. His blue eyes glowed like twin sapphires in his deeply tanned face. "Cricket, maybe I'm doing you an injustice, but our winters *are* hard and long. You're not staying just to prove to me you can, are you?" He looked faintly ashamed and she sensed the importance of her answer.

"I was at first," she admitted and felt her face color down to the slightly rounded neckline of the cotton gown she wore. "Now —" she spread her hands. "Loring, my parents died when I was small. I never had anyone but Gramps. Maybe that's why I couldn't take a chance with his health and go ahead and enroll in nurse's training when I wanted to." She caught his look of surprise and rushed on. "You can't know what it means for me to be part of a real family, not just live with Gramps, servants, and company. After Mary came with little Barney I knew how much I'd missed." A forlorn note crept into her voice.

"Out here are things I can't buy with money. Maybe that's why I find them priceless." She pointed out the window to the distant mountains. "I've also found out how satisfying it is to work and see the results in a clean house or a good meal." Her voice lowered. "I-I've also thought a lot about God and what you said that day last summer." A wave of shyness overcame her.

Loring's face took on a radiance that left Cricket gasping. Every picture of Sir Galahad and Sir Lancelot she had seen in storybooks paled before the beauty of his expression, the unguarded look in his eyes. "I know. I've seen you studying the Bible. I'm praying for you." With a quick clasp of her hand, he whispered, "Good night," and disappeared down the hall.

I belong here, with him and with his God.

Cricket flinched from the thought and tore upstairs. Her hand tingled from his strong touch. Never had she felt for Cliff or anyone else the feelings churning inside. "Don't be ridiculous," she admonished herself. "He's not of your world. You're not of his." Yet was that true? She no longer fit in what had been her world, and the world Loring Ames lived in had become dearer to her than anything she had known. "Loring's qualifications," as she had often reminded herself, came to mind, his recipe for a happy marriage: a girl who loved God, loved Loring, and could be his pard.

Well, if the depth of her feelings accurately portrayed love, she met that test. More and more she was learning to be a pard. That left the most important thing, "as dedicated to God and His Son the Lord

Jesus Christ as I am," Loring had said. Cricket shivered. Even if she could know God and Jesus, did her shallow upbringing enable her to ever become such a woman?

"He said he was praying for me," she whispered. A new thought brought her to the windows, seeking wisdom and knowledge from the friendly stars. Loring would pray for anyone attempting to find his Lord, but even though he'd quickly covered the telltale expression in his eyes, love had been there.

10

"I don't know these authors, Martha." Cricket looked helplessly at the well-stocked shelves. "Pick out a book for me, will you? I like reading the Bible but I guess right now I'm in the mood for something else."

Martha reached to the shelf above her head. "Try these."

"Emilie Loring. I never heard of her." Cricket fingered their crisp, new-smelling dust jackets.

"She only has the two out so far. Read *The Trail of Conflict* first, it's her first book. *Here Comes the Sun* just came out recently." Martha laughed. "I guess I was attracted first because of her name, at least that's what Loring says. But Mrs. Loring is an excellent writer. She never preaches but her characters have high ideals. You'll like the books. Besides, *The Trail of Conflict* has some elements in it you'll relate to well."

A few hours later an ecstatic Cricket finished the book. Her eyes burned with enjoyment. During those hours she had lived the story of Geraldine Courtlandt, a society girl much like herself, who came West and found danger, love, and excitement as well as a literal trail of conflict.

Almost in a daze, Cricket compared the story with her own life and sighed. Gerry had to face a lot of misunderstanding and living before finding happiness. How much would a transplanted Cricket be forced to endure to find her own hearth? Her face warmed when Loring Ames's steady gaze rose to her mind.

Perhaps the secret knowledge she hugged to herself and the spell of the romance worked together to promote disaster. In any event, Cricket momentarily reverted to the I'll-have-what-I-want when-I-want-it mood she'd almost overcome since working her way on Tillicum Ranch.

It started when Gramps and Loring unaccountably disappeared and she saw them riding off into the mountains. "Why didn't they take me?" she asked Martha indignantly. "I've been wanting to ride but Loring said it looked too stormy. Now just look at them."

Martha frowned. "I heard Charles ask Loring to take him. He said it was important." Her floury hands stilled on the bread

175

board. "It surprised me that Loring would go in this weather."

"Gramps can be persuasive." But Cricket's ruffled feathers didn't subside. "Where are they going, anyway?"

"Maybe Charles wanted to see the old corral." She smiled. "Cricket, how would you like to read something I wrote a long time ago when I was boarding away from home during the week?"

Hurt feelings forgotten, Cricket swung away from the window. "I didn't know you wrote."

"I don't, really. This was something I did for fun a long time ago." She washed her hands, dried them, and led Cricket to the library. Martha took down a heavy wooden box and removed several sheets of paper. "Before I met Bill I taught school in a small mountain town not far from here, the hamlet in which I grew up. When Bill was courting me, I got a lot of teasing, especially from my brothers and sisters and step-father." Her eyes softened with memories. "Funny things happened then too. One of the funniest was the story of Bill and his team." She handed over the faded pages. "Read it while I punch the bread down. You see, Bill had agreed to be a deacon in the church play." She smiled again and left Cricket with the poem.

BILL AND HIS TEAM

Listen, my people, and you shall know
A curious tale of the long ago.
Remember this story, and learn it well . . .
It sometime may help you,
    you never can tell.

Up in the mountains, in a small town
A number of dwellings were scattered
    around.
But off to one side,
    surrounded by woods
The home of "Rube" Cole,
    the old logger stood.

Rube had a stepdaughter,
    a schoolma'am of old,
By her profession she made heaps
    of gold.
Ed was the brother, long, lanky, and
    lean
You'd never forget him if him
    once you'd seen.

Now Rube had to work about eight miles
    from home
But on Saturday night,
    back he would come
To stay with his family until Sunday eve

For that was the time he always
    must leave.

Then there was Bill, a deacon-to-be
Who came every Sunday
    the schoolma'am to see.
He had a fine team, the best in the town
He and Miss Martha would oft
    ride around.

He'd come up and get her on Sunday eve
Then take her back when she
    had to leave
While the team would stand
    at the little gate
And wait for the "deacon,"
    sometimes quite late.
For until after church they sometimes
    would stay
And have their supper before going away.

One bright afternoon instead of walking
    back down
Dad said to Ed, "Let's just stick around.
"I've been thinking . . . how much better
    'twould seem
To hitch us a ride with Bill
    and his team."

The afternoon waned, but they

didn't mind,
Many folks passed, but they
    stayed behind.
"Why should we care, we have
    a fine scheme,
We're going tonight with Bill and his team."

The evening went by and also the fun,
They got in the rig and went on the run.
Things went quite smoothly
    a few miles or so
Then one old horse seemed to say,
    "I don't want to go!"
Slower and slower they went with
    the load,
Till that horse lay down in the middle
    of the road!
    Dad looked at Ed, and Ed looked
        at me,
    Bill looked at one, and then at
        all three.

"We'll soon fix it up," the "deacon" said,
So he jumped right out by the old
    horse's head.
"Get up there, fellow," we heard
    him say . . .
But there in the road he continued to lay.
As Bill looked puzzled and scratched
    his dome

We caught his faint words ". . . and
    four miles from home!"
    But to stand there and gaze got
      us nowhere at all
    Just wishing that horse was home in
      his stall.

Bill took his head and Dad took his tail,
It seemed to me they just couldn't fail
The way that they pulled it seemed like
    a cinch,
But no sir, that old horse never budged
    one inch!

Dad looked at Ed, and Ed looked at me,
Bill looked at one, and then at all three.
They took off the harness and unhitched
    the cart,
They then got ready for another start.

Bill at the head, Dad at the tail,
Ed took the mane . . . they just
    couldn't fail!
By now we all knew we were in
    a tight pinch,
    Still . . . the old critter never budged
      one inch!

The rain pattered down and Dad said,
    "Let's roam

Before we get wet . . . for we're four miles
    from home."
Then once more they tried the old horse
    to move
Two said they'd pull while the other one
    shoved.

How hard they all worked, there was
    barely a sound
And to all our surprise he stood up
    on the ground.
But he was just too sick to hold
    up his head,
"We'll leave him here,"
    the "deacon" said.
"Perhaps when he's better he'll
    follow us home,
At any rate, we'll not force him to come."
    We pulled the big cart out
      of everyone's way
And there by the roadside we said
    he could stay.

We started our journey, right straight
    down the road,
Carrying enough to make quite a load.
First came old Doll, the horse
    faithful and true
Next came Dad, back a step or two.
Then came Ed, lean, lanky, and long,

It seemed we could hear him humming
    a song.
The words that he sang only few
    I could tell
They were "just like a gypsy"
    and fitted us well.

Next after Ed, the "deacon" came,
Poor old fellow was awfully lame.
You cannot wonder from the load
    that he carried,
I bet he wished he were dead and buried!

Then in the rear the schoolma'am
    was seen,
The way that she giggled, it surely
    was mean!
But all of the laughter pent up
    to this time
Suddenly burst forth as she viewed
    the long line
        Trudging so bravely along in the rain
        They looked all the world like gypsies
            from Spain.

Straight down the road we continued
    to roam
At last we could say, "Only three miles
    from home.
By keeping right on to the goal we

must come,"
And by following this maxim,
    we finally reached home.

Poor old Dynamite remained in the rear
We no more that night did his
    gentle whinny hear.

'Twas not very long before each
    was in bed
While visions of cart wrecks danced
    in our heads.
But we heard Dad murumur in the midst
    of his dream,
"Next time *I* don't wait for Bill
    and his team."

Cricket ran laughing to the kitchen. "Martha, what happened? About Dynamite and how did your stepfather and brother get to work?"

She looked disgusted but her merry eyes betrayed her. "Dynamite was back in the barn at their home across the river before Bill got there. Dad and Ed had to get up before dawn even considered cracking and hike those eight miles to work." A gentle smile lit up her face. "It's shared memories like those that make marriage rich." She glanced out the window at the darkening sky. "I wish Loring and Charles would come back."

Yet two hours passed before the two wearily dismounted. Charles looked pleased; Loring did not. Cricket's grudge at being left behind returned and she refused to mention it. After supper Gramps did.

"You ought to see that old cabin and corral, Cricket," he blandly stated. "You know, where Bill and Martha lived when they first got married. It's really something. Loring, why don't you take her tomorrow before it snows?" He described the interior, the snug roof, and the well-stocked shelves in case a line rider got caught out overnight. Cricket burned with anger. Loring knew she wanted to go.

"I will. Tomorrow."

"Not with a blizzard coming on," Big Bill protested and Loring nodded.

"If you don't want to go *again*," she stressed the word and lifted her chin. "I'll go alone. I can follow the tracks you made today."

"Better wait until spring," Martha advised but Cricket had the bit in her mouth and wouldn't back down.

"No, I'm going. Tomorrow."

Bill shrugged. "If she's dead set on it you'll have to take her."

"I know." Loring glanced at Gramps. Was he angry with the older man for praising the trip with a storm coming?

Cricket shivered when she got in bed that night. She almost regretted her decision. On the other hand, not a drop of snow fell. In the morning, bundled into the heaviest clothing she owned, she mounted Buckskin. Loring silently vaulted into Bay's saddle and they rode off on the well-marked trail toward the distant mountains and old cabin with Bill, Martha, and a subdued Gramps waving from the shelter of the wide front porch.

Once out of sight of the house Cricket's spirits rose. If Gramps could make it to the cabin and back so could she. She couldn't resist telling Loring, "You don't have to go if you don't want to." When he tightened his lips and obstinately stayed silent she taunted, "If you and Gramps had taken me yesterday we wouldn't be making this trip." He didn't respond. Her patience came to an end.

"If you weren't going to talk to me, why did you come?" This time her stinging words brought results, but they only added fuel to the fire of her indignation.

"When children insist on having their own way, a grownup has to be along to look after them." In an instant he seemed to regret his words. The respect, friendship, and trust that had grown between them since the previous summer was torn down by his curt reply. Cricket turned her head away to hide the angry tears that sprang to her eyes, but set her lips and kept riding straight ahead. So that was how he thought of her, she thought bitterly. A spoiled child. Deep inside she admitted she had acted that way about the ride today, but after all, if he would take Gramps, why not her?

The farther they went the thicker the snowflakes became. Cricket wished she had the nerve to suggest turning back. Bill Ames had been right, a real blizzard was coming up. But she only set her stubborn chin higher.

Once she had told Loring in a voice about as warm as an icicle, "If the snow bothers you or if you're afraid of getting caught out in the storm you can always go back, you know."

But Loring's face was grim, "It's too late to turn back now, much too late." There was a note in his voice that caused Cricket to shiver, and not from the cold. The going was getting rougher. She felt sorry for Buckskin and Bay, trying to plow through the snow that even in this short time had managed to pile into towering drifts. She had never known how hard it could snow. Then, too, as they rode higher and higher to the mountain cabin, they encountered not only fresh snow but snow that had evidently fallen in the night.

"Was there snow when you and Gramps were here yesterday?" If Loring hadn't been so intent on making a way, checking signs to be sure they were on the right trail, he might have noticed the little tremor in her voice. Cricket was getting tired and cold. *Why had she insisted on this trip?*

"Not like this." His answer was short. "It snowed all last night up here. There's not a trace of our tracks from yesterday. It must have snowed over a foot just last night and another two or three inches this morning." How could he see through the growing gloom? The flakes stung Cricket's face. This was nothing like being inside a comfortable New York home watching out the window while the flakes fell. This was miserable and frightening. Well, at least she was with a capable guide.

"I'm glad you didn't let me come alone." Her impulsive words sounded hollow against the increasing storm. But Loring's answer was steady and typical.

"That would never happen." A slight

trickle of warmth stole into Cricket's heart. Maybe he would forgive her for this dumb stunt. If only she had not forced him to come!

"The cabin isn't far ahead." Loring had to lean close to her to make himself heard. The storm had begun howling until it seemed a thousand devils had been loosed on the mountainside. Great trees with their weight of white bent low to the ground. The wind shrieked through their tops, lifting snow, swirling it into mists and drifts. Never had Cricket seen such madness. Could nature be like this? Although she was naturally brave, this was something to frighten the hardiest soul. She could tell by the gravity of Loring's face he wished they were safely at home.

Silently she followed the path he and Bay were making. It was such hard going! Loring had dismounted now, trying to save his horse. But when Cricket prepared to do the same he waved for her to stay where she was. She sensed his concern as to whether she could hold in Buckskin in this storm if she were on foot. Suddenly in the midst of the storm there was a scream beyond description. Was it a woman screaming in the dusk, crying for help? Buckskin reared and instantly Cricket clutched the reins, bringing him down. But almost before she could realize the danger, another scream came.

Loring dropped the reins of his own horse. His shouted command for Bay to stay was swept away on the wind. Expert as Cricket was with horses, she would never be able to handle Buckskin when he heard the screams of a cougar. The terrified horse reared again, but Loring was there.

"Down, down!" He grabbed the bridle, forcing Buckskin down just as the third horrendous scream split the storm. Buckskin stood nervously, panting with fright, but before Loring could get back to Bay the horse had bolted, running as rapidly as he could back down the path they had just broken.

"Oh, no!" Cricket closed her eyes against the realization of their predicament. "Can you catch him?" She bent low to whisper to Loring. But the snow-covered figure only shook his head. "Not in this storm. A horse terrified by a cougar will run for miles. Besides, I can't leave you here." The words were flat, deliberate. "Come." He took the reins from her, faced into the storm, and with a still trembling Buckskin close behind once more began breaking trail.

"Thank God for his superb strength." Had she spoken aloud? Cricket didn't know. It wouldn't have mattered if she had. Words were snatched as soon as spoken and carelessly flung into the storm. Although it was not yet noon, the storm had brought a dusky gloom that made the day look spent. How much farther? Cricket's hands and feet felt frozen. What had possessed her to get them into this? If anything happened to Loring it would be her fault. She shivered and looked over her shoulder. Did cougars attack people?

In the time it took to get to the cabin Cricket had a chance to reflect. Never had she been in such physical danger, facing a storm. Never had she been out facing the elements, dependent totally on the knowledge of another human being. What if she were alone? Or for that matter, what if she were with any one of her own crowd? Suddenly all the shallow, surface values began to shift. Those who had looked down on this man would have given up, been lost hours ago. In spite of his familiarity with the mountains Cricket couldn't see how even Loring could keep going. Yet he faced straight ahead, never varying. He couldn't see more than a foot ahead. How could he be so sure they were on the right track, or any track at all?

I wonder why I'm not more afraid. Strangely enough, once the cougar's screams had stopped, Cricket had calmed down a bit. She had a feeling she would be protected. In spite of the grueling trek she had full confidence in Loring's ability. If anyone could get them to that cabin he could. Gradually the storm receded from her consciousness. She was no longer afraid. She was just so cold she was numb. It was all she could do to hold on and not slide off Buckskin. What if her fingers loosened from her grip? Did it really matter? She had heard freezing to death was fairly painless. But she didn't want to die! With a mighty effort she roused herself from the lethargy the storm and cold had brought on. Buckskin had stopped. Where was Loring?

"Loring!" In an instant he was beside her, lifting her bodily from the saddle. For the first time she noticed Buckskin was tied, tied to a porch rail! A porch rail?

They had reached the cabin! Loring was hurrying her through the door, hastily throwing shavings and wood into a fireplace, touching a match to them. The warmth of the fire began to thaw Cricket's very bones, but how her fingers and toes ached when they began to come to life. Loring had unceremoniously pulled off her boots and thick socks, massaging her poor, frozen feet. Tears of pain slipped down Cricket's face, but she uttered no sound.

And yet it wasn't so long before she was warm, at least her hands and feet. Loring had left her to go into another small room. Now he came back carrying an armful of garments. A woolly sweater. A pair of overalls. Thick, warm, dry socks.

"Get into them while I take care of Buckskin," he advised. Cricket was only too glad to follow his order. The sweater was miles too big, but over her own blouse which had managed to stay dry under her coat it wasn't too bad. The overalls were only slightly too large. They must have been Loring's when he was a teen-ager or even younger. She found a belt that cinched them in enough and pulled the long dry socks on. Never in all her days of beautiful clothing had Cricket appreciated anything as much as those shabby clothes! Glancing around the cabin she spied an Indian blanket, clean but frayed. In spite of the sweater she was still cold, so padding across the floor in the thick socks she grabbed the blanket, wrapped it around her, and curled up in the old rocker by the blazing fire.

With the door closed and the fire crackling, some of the storm was shut out. Yet she had to face the seriousness of her own selfish determination to do what she pleased. They had one horse and the storm showed no signs of abating. There was no way, even with Loring's ability, for them to get back to Tillicum that day. *Her reputation!* What would happen if the newspapers ever got wind that she, Charity Endicott, had spent the night in a lonely Wyoming mountain cabin with a strapping guide?

There was only one thing to do. As soon as Loring came in she would tell him. She didn't have long to wait. He came in stamping snow, looking rather pleased with himself. Seeing her astonishment he grinned outright, his wet hair hanging down over his face.

"Buckskin's bedded down. We keep the old stable in good repair. There's plenty of feed for him, even if we have to stay a week." Cricket couldn't believe her ears.

"A week?"

"Sure," he told her cheerfully, opening cupboards in the kitchen part of the big room. "Blizzards often last a week in this country."

"I can't stay here with you!" His eyes narrowed as he spun around.

"And just where do you think you're going?" By now she had flung off the blanket and was reaching for her boots that he had propped in front of the fire and that were steaming dry.

"I'll follow Bay's trail and send help back for you." Even as she said it Cricket realized how ridiculous the suggestion was. She could no more find her way back than she could fly. But the look in his face made her even more determined. He was struggling to keep from laughing.

"Oh, all right," she conceded. "You take Buckskin and leave me here. There's plenty of food. Even if you can't get back until tomorrow I'll be fine." This time Loring Ames laughed out loud.

"My dear Miss Endicott," he said with all of the old mockery in his voice. There was even a devil-may-care glint in his blue eyes. If Cricket had known him better she would have seen that once this man had to face something, the decision was made and abided by and there was no turning back.

"My dear Miss Endicott," he repeated, "no one is going anywhere in this storm." He ignored her outraged gasp. "I'm afraid you're stuck with me, or perhaps I should say we're stuck with each other."

"You mean we have to stay here *together?*"

"That's exactly what I mean." There was a deadly finality in his words, but Cricket didn't hear them for what they were. Instantly she was on her feet.

"That's impossible, you know that! What will people say?" He was watching her closely.

"You needn't worry. You won't be bothered." A wave of red covered her face and she lifted her chin haughtily.

"I know that. You've made it perfectly clear you have no use for me. But what will everyone think? They'll never believe it was an accident, our being up here!"

"Accident? It was no accident." Cricket's heart lurched. What did he mean?

"Did you plan this?" This time his laughter almost drowned out the muffled sounds of the storm. He fairly rocked with it as she stood there indignantly holding her ground, a slightly ridiculous figure in the too-large sweater and faded overalls, sock-covered feet planted firmly in front of the hearth.

"At the risk of sounding, shall I say, rather unchivalrous, may I remind you it was not *I* who insisted on this little trip . . ." In that moment she hated him. His unfinished sentence was filled with meaning.

"Of all the . . ." Cricket was so furious she couldn't go on.

"Oh, it's all right. I don't feel my good name will be compromised. After all, I'm sure you didn't know just how bad the storm would be." He went back to the cupboards, setting supplies on the table, ignoring her rage as she stared at his back.

In the game of life seldom had Cricket been completely routed. But to think this, this, this, she stuttered mentally, this country bumpkin would have the gall to stand there, and . . .

"Come on and help, will you? We're in this together." How did he dare? Never had she seen such audacity.

"I'm not hungry." It was a lie. Her stomach was clamoring for something to eat.

"Well, I am. Get some dinner ready. I have to bring in some more wood." He stepped through a smaller door near the kitchen cupboards that evidently led to some kind of woodshed. In a moment he was back, his hands full, and in a few more minutes had a good fire going in the old-fashioned wood stove.

He expected her to cook for him, and on that monstrosity! In silence she watched as he refastened his jacket and stepped back outside. This time he was gone longer. When he came back in it was with a large tin bucket of water. Setting it on the homemade table he turned toward her, disarming her with his smile.

"Look, Cricket. Neither of us would have

chosen this. But there really is no other alternative. We can't get out of here, either of us," he emphasized the words. "We'll have to ride out the storm. Bay will go back to the ranch, but it may take a lot longer than we think. When he does they can get out and come for us. Until then they'll know we have a horse and plenty of food. But if we're fighting all the time this is going to be unbearable." He paused but her stony silence told him nothing.

"All right, then. I'll be busy getting wood and water and checking on Buckskin. You can cook, you know you can. Ever since you came here you've been trying to prove that you could make it in this country. Now's your chance. This is the same cabin, the same stove, the same everything my mom started with. Can't you look on it as a kind of challenge? With roads clogged with snow, which they will be, there won't be any traffic to the ranch. No one ever needs to know we were trapped up here except my folks and Gramps.

"But even if they did, so what? Is it really any worse than some of the jaunts you city people take together without what my mom would call a good old-fashioned chaperone? I've already told you you won't be bothered. Besides, I've always felt that those who are your friends don't believe bad things . . . who cares about the rest of them? God knows where we are and that you're in no danger."

It was the longest speech Cricket had ever heard him make. She could see his logic, but her heart smarted at the thought of public opinion. She had always hated any suggestion of compromise. Yet, as he said, there was no alternative. For a long time she stared at him, then finally a small smile curled about her lips.

"Okay, boss. What do I do first?"

11

Because of the snow, the little mountain cabin grew dark early. Loring and Cricket ate ravenously of the good lunch brought from Tillicum and washed it down with steaming coffee.

Cricket suddenly laughed. Now with no choice remaining but to stay, why make a tragedy of it? Funny. Loring Ames was the only man she knew she would trust in such a situation. Loring's fire-building capabilities and the yellow glow from a kerosene lamp lent charm to the rude cabin and the patch-work quilts on the built-in bunks reminded her how Loring's parents had actually lived here years before.

Loring's eyes sparkled in the lamplight and his lips curved in an answering smile. "I'm glad you can laugh."

Without considering the effect of her words, Cricket laughed again and said, "I'm just sitting here being glad you're the one I'm with and not Barney Delevan."

Every trace of amusement fled from her companion's face. His eyes flashed and darkened like the summer sky before a bad storm. Contempt turned down the corners of his mouth. "So am I." He silently rose and shrugged into his heavy coat. "There's hot water on the stove. If you'll do the dishes I'll check on Buckskin once more before it's too dark." He lit an old but well cared for lantern and eased open the door against the storm, leaving Cricket biting her tongue, wishing she could recall her careless words.

Snowy wind whistled around the cabin the moment Loring stepped outside. Cricket shivered. What if he had let her come alone? She cringed at the thought. A warm rush of appreciation blotted out her fear. Loring would take care of her. She drew in a ragged breath. She must do her part, too.

When he came in, all traces of anger had been left outside in the night. They settled in rude but comfortable handmade chairs before the fire and Cricket said, "I wonder if you appreciate your parents as much as you should." He looked surprised but she rushed on. "Until we came out here Gramps and I were close but he didn't have all that much time for me, especially before he had the bad spells." She stared into the flames.

"That's why I just couldn't go into nursing when he opposed it so much." She sighed. "I did learn a lot taking care of him, though."

Loring maintained a sympathetic silence and Cricket yawned. "Guess this day's about done me in."

He instantly rose. "Are you sure you're dry and warm?" He eyed the woolly sweater, worn socks, and overalls he'd provided earlier. "Your own clothes aren't dry yet. You'll have to sleep in those."

"Good." She huddled deeper into the old sweater and obediently uncurled herself from her chair. "Right or left?"

"Right or left what?"

"Bunk. Which is mine?" The unorthodox situation they shared brought color to her face but it subsided when Loring told her, "It doesn't matter. They're identical except for quilts. Which do you like best?"

"The red and white one." She yawned until she felt her jaw might dislocate and stumbled across the room. Thirty seconds later she lay inside a nest of warm blankets that smelled of wood smoke and the next thing she knew gray daylight had sneaked in through a crude window. Content to stay where she was, Cricket noted the carefully made bunk Loring must have occupied. She stretched in the warm air from the cheerful fires in the fireplace and unwieldy cook stove and then slid from bed and quickly made use of the pan of warm water, bar of soap, and clean towel on a bench nearby. She had just finished getting the tangles from her hair with a small comb she always carried, glad for the shortness of her curls, when a soft knock and a low voice calling her name roused her.

"Here, Loring." She flung the door wide and stepped back from the snow-covered figure almost invisible behind the enormous armload of wood he carried and dumped near the fireplace.

"Morning." His dark gold hair looked frosted. Rivulets from melting snowflakes creased his tanned face but he also appeared rested. "Are you hungry?"

"Starved." Her lips turned up in an answering smile and her heart soared. The same quickly guarded look she'd seen in his eyes once before softened their blueness and quickly fled. "What's for breakfast? Shall I cook?"

"Please. I need to pack in a lot more wood." Some of his joy dwindled. "We're in for a bad spell."

Cricket rummaged in the supplies. "Here's flour and salt and —" her voice got lost in the small cupboard. "I can make biscuits and here are canned peaches and canned meat with gravy. Is it beef?"

"Venison. Miss Endicott, your breakfast menu sounds good."

She tossed him an unreadable glance over one shoulder and reached for a pan. "Endicott's Eatery strives to please." But the up-to-date stove at Tillicum and the beast in the cabin bore little resemblance to one another. This oven didn't heat evenly and while the center biscuits turned out delicious, the ones at one end scorched and those at the other remained underdone and doughy.

"Throw out the burned ones, put the palefaces back in, and we'll start with the middle ones," Loring directed. "First, we'll return thanks." He bowed his head. Cricket hastily followed suit. "Father, we thank You for this food and for keeping us safe. May we ever live according to Your will. For Jesus' sake, Amen."

Cricket caught her breath at the look in his eyes when he reopened them and smiled at her. Breathless, she jumped up from the small table she'd set for two. "I-I'll check on the other biscuits." This time they had browned correctly and, more biscuits than she cared to admit to later, she sat back filled and again content.

All morning Loring packed in gigantic loads of wood. Cricket found a broom, dampened it, and swept the rude floor. She took stock of the well-supplied cupboard, cocked her head to one side, and decided that stew and the rest of the biscuits would do for supper. When she discovered several quarts of sliced apples her face lit up. Did she dare try an apple pie on her own? Why not? She'd surprise Loring with her newly gained culinary skills.

In spite of the continuing snow, she hummed while she worked. "There's a long, long trail . . ." The song had been so popular during the war. What had it been like to have a loved one far away and in danger? Her sticky hands stilled in the pie dough. What if she had known Loring then and had been forced to wait, wondering as his parents and thousands of others, not knowing where or how their sons were?

She shivered and suddenly realized Loring had been gone a long time and the fire in the fireplace had turned sullen.

"Keep the home fires burning!" She laughed and piled wood on the way she had seen Loring do. She restocked the kitchen stove too. That black beast ate wood like locusts ate crops.

Cricket opened the door and heard Buckskin whinny. Relief filled her. Loring must be caring for the faithful horse.

She quickly shut the door, noting that the temperature had dropped, and rubbed her arms and went back to her pie. Yet a certain uneasiness stole over her and as soon as she got the pie in the oven she opened the door again and called, "Loring!"

Only white silence replied.

"Loring?" Alarm grew. Surely he wouldn't go out of hearing in this weather!

Buckskin whinnied again. Heedless of the fact her now-dry coat hung over a chair, Cricket ran outside and toward the old corral. She slipped and slid in the deep snow, only half-conscious of snow filling her boots, pelting down on her uncovered head, and blurring her vision. She reached the rude shelter that housed Buckskin and slipped inside, almost falling over a prone figure on the ground at her feet.

"Loring!" The storm muffled her scream. She knelt and shook him. Her hands came away red and slippery. Fresh blood.

The world reeled. "Dear God!"

She tried to lift him but could not. Her fingers trembled but a strange voice she knew must be hers ordered, "Settle down. You have to help him. Head wounds bleed profusely. Remember what everyone knows and *get that blood stopped.*"

Why hadn't she grabbed a scarf, anything, to staunch the red flow staining the straw close to Buckskin's nervous feet? Her frantic gaze shifted to the horse and his saddle blanket. "Sorry, old boy. I'll bring you another from the cabin later." But the tough material wouldn't tear. She rapidly tucked the blanket around Loring and jerked his jacket open to feel for his heart. Its steady beating reassured her and with a cry of triumph she snatched at his knotted neckerchief, managed to get it undone in spite of slowly freezing fingers, and wadded it into a pad. She pressed it hard against the cut forehead, relieved to find the wound was actually a shallow furrow.

"Then why is he unconscious?" she demanded of Buckskin and ran her fingers around his head. Her heart sank. A large bump had grown there. Was his skull fractured? Or had he just been knocked out?

She checked the neckerchief bandage and discovered the bleeding had stopped. Cold bit into her bones. She must get Loring inside. Could she rouse him enough to enlist his help?

Again her gaze traveled the cramped space. "Good!" A bucket of water stood nearby. No ice. Loring must have fetched it for Buckskin not long ago. Cricket's teeth chattered when she thrust in both hands, cupped them, and dashed the freezing water into Loring's face. He didn't open his eyes but a faint groan lit a candle of hope in the girl's heart.

"Loring, you have to help me. God, You, too." With incredible strength she helped him stand and screamed again, "Help me, God! Loring, *walk!*" Step by step, her arms around him, her slender shoulders bent under his weight, she managed to stagger toward the cabin and inside. "Just a few steps more," she pleaded with the half-conscious man.

"Thank God!" She tumbled him onto his bunk, sank to the floor beside him to catch her breath, and bit back sobs of fear.

The smell of burning pie crust roused her. She ran to the oven and turned the pie. Only a tiny piece of crust had burned. She broke it off and noticed steam rising from the hot water on top of the stove. "I have to clean the wound," she muttered. "Surely a refuge like this must have some kind of medicine in case of injury." By the time she found a small box containing gauze, ointment, and alcohol every bone in her body ached. She doggedly refused to rest. If only she had taken nurse's training!

"Well, you didn't," she snapped to herself, nerves raw. "So use your common sense. Wash out that wound and do the best you can." Her fingers warmed in the water and she gently made a soapy lather and washed the furrow. It took three tries to adjust a bandage made from strips of gauze after she smothered the wound with ointment and padded it. Loring had begun to show signs of returning consciousness. She must fix the bandage firmly enough so he wouldn't work it loose. At least the skin hadn't broken on that alarming bump.

Cricket wracked her brain to remember. Oh yes, weren't you supposed to make persons with bumps like that walk, in case they had a concussion? She sighed and got Loring awake enough to drape his arm over her shoulders again. Up and down. Back and forth until she nearly collapsed. A pot of strong hot coffee helped. She drank hers straight and managed to get some down him. She also buried him in blankets. How long had he lain there in the cold? It couldn't have been too long. His skin remained cool but not freezing and an hour later his breathing appeared more normal, as if he'd fallen into a natural sleep.

Unwilling to stop to cook, she stuffed herself on warm apple pie and thought bitterly how it had been to surprise Loring. "Stop it." Cricket's command sounded loud in the quiet room. "You have a lot to do here, so stop acting like a baby."

She glanced around the room. No problem with wood, at least for a time. Besides, a great stack lay in the shed next to Buckskin if she needed it.

What else? Water. If it snowed much more she couldn't reach the outside pump. She remembered how Loring melted snow and said he'd pour it on the pump to get it started. Cricket bundled up and raced to the pump, unconsciously praying, "God, please let it work." It did. She filled every kettle and pan she could find except one frying pan. She could always cook in it if she had to. She also remembered to get the lariat that always hung on Buckskin's saddle horn and tie one end to a nail outside the cabin, the other to the post of Buckskin's shelter. She spied a shovel in the shed and carried it back to the cabin feeling she'd unearthed a treasure greater than all the jewels she once wore.

To think that a few hours ago she had been thinking only of her reputation! She allowed a smile of contempt for her former self but now her worry was to stay alive and care for Loring. She must keep the fires burning, be sure Buckskin stayed warm and fed, and get enough rest so she didn't grow ill.

For three endless days the blizzard reigned over the mountain cabin. For three days Loring never regained consciousness enough to recognize her. Cricket toiled and prayed, hoping that the God she had ignored would hear her petitions for the sake of His child, Loring. Tempted to promise God that if Loring pulled through she'd serve Him forever tugged at her mind but she couldn't do it. How did one bargain with God?

The morning of the fourth day brought relief. Cricket awakened to sunlight and hope — until she peered out. Never had she seen more beauty, or cruelty. Snow had drifted into monstrous, glistening shapes. Icicles as thick as her waist hung from the eaves. It took her over an hour to make a path wide enough for her to reach Buckskin, who nickered his loneliness, in spite of staying well fed from the generous supply Cricket had remembered to leave near. He drank thirstily of the melted snow water she brought and tears filled the girl's eyes. "I'm glad you're here, boy." She reached the cabin. Loring was burning up. Was there infection in the wound after all? She had thought it was healing so nicely . . . or was it something else?

Cricket was about at the end of her rope. Would someone come that day? But the day dragged on, hour after weary hour. She bathed Loring's face in cold water and sponged off his neck and arms. She didn't dare give him a complete sponge bath, the cabin never warmed up enough. If he developed pneumonia, what would she do then? Once when she went to the cupboard for supplies she caught sight of herself in a small mirror stuck against the chinked log wall.

Was that really her own face looking back? It was pale, wan, and sick looking. She'd better force herself to eat or she'd be next on the sick list. Gradually Loring's fever subsided and by evening his temperature was only slightly above normal. He even opened his eyes once. Their restless gaze sought her, but she shook her head and placed her finger on his lips. He mustn't try to talk, not yet.

For the last few nights she had not slept much, tossing and turning, wondering if her pitiful efforts could do enough to save him. In case he awoke or groaned in the night she wanted to be there. Long after midnight her weary body refused to continue and she fell into a troubled sleep. She was awakened by Loring sitting straight up in bed, wild-eyed, ranting and raving.

"I can't do it Charles, I can't do it! . . . She will hate me . . . The telegram? . . . No . . . Keep her there? . . . Yes, I love her!" A great thrill shot through the listening girl. Loring was delirious, but was he speaking about her? She didn't have time to analyze the joy in her heart. Dipping a cloth into the icy water in the pan beside her she washed his face. It settled him down a bit, but his rambling went on.

"The telegram . . . yes. *How could she?*" There was a long silence, then, "All right, Charles." The voice was old, defeated. "How get her there? . . . God forgive you . . ." The rest was lost in a mumble. Finally Cricket managed to get him settled down again. Long after he was asleep she sat staring, trying to figure out what his disjointed speech meant. What was it Gramps wanted Loring to do that he didn't want to do? What was that about a telegram? Bit by bit small pieces of the puzzle fell into place until at last she thought she had it figured out.

First of all, there must have been a telegram, an upsetting one. But from whom?

Did it really matter? In a flash the level look of understanding that had passed between Loring and Gramps the night before she and Loring came to the cabin stood before her eyes. What had Loring said?

"Yes, I will have to go with her." She hadn't thought anything of it at the time. Now it came back to haunt her. It began to dawn on her how reluctant Loring had been to come. How he and her grandfather had spent the previous day at the cabin, leaving her at home. How Gramps had deliberately praised the place, encouraging her to go, and to go the very next day. Had it all been part of a plan?

With sudden insight Cricket began to see more and more. She wouldn't put it past Gramps to plan something just like this. But what force had he brought to bear on Loring to execute it? How neatly she had fallen into the little trap! She had insisted on coming. How Gramps must have enjoyed that. He had probably paid Loring to bring her up here and keep her a few days, thinking it would be a good lesson. What about the Ameses? Were they *all* in on it?

Cricket faced it squarely. If they were all in on it, then there would be no hope of rescue. Unless . . . her spirits brightened. Bay would go home, they would know something was wrong. But as her weary eyes shut once more Loring's words flashed back, ". . . Bay will go back to the ranch, but it may take a lot longer than we think." Another groan from the sick man brought her wide awake once more, awake to tangle with the raging storm in her soul.

12

The blizzard that had stranded Loring and Cricket in the mountain cabin had raged in the valley as well. The first day or two Gramps had delighted in it, almost crowing as he walked from window to window looking at the great drifts. But as it went on, into the third and fourth days he began to get a haunted look in his eyes. Martha noticed it first, then Bill. More and more he stood by the window, looking out. Bill tried to cheer him up.

"Don't worry about Cricket, Charles. Loring will take care of her." He idly knit his fingers together. "I still can't understand why you encouraged her to go. You must have known the blizzard was coming, we all told you." There was reproach in his voice.

He had no fear for Loring. He and Loring had been out in worse storms than this and often holed up in the cabin to wait them out. But what would it be like for Cricket, alone in a strange cabin, walled in with the snow, knowing the harm that could be done her reputation if the story ever trickled out to the waiting ears of a gossipy world?

Charles didn't have an answer. He was doing some tall thinking himself. He *had* known it was going to snow, it was one of the things he had counted on. Suddenly he whirled from the window, determination on his face. His voice was husky and there was an ashamed look on his face.

"I think I'd better tell you the whole thing." He looked strange, frightened. Martha and Bill looked up in surprise. Whatever could he mean?

"I asked Loring to get her up there and keep her a few days."

"You *what?*" There was something terrible in the usual kindly voice of Bill Ames. His blue eyes so like his son's flashed. This man facing him had dared . . .

"Wait. Before you judge me too harshly, look at this." He slowly pulled a crumpled yellow telegram from his pocket. From its looks, it must have been in Charles's possession several days. "You were all outside when the message came. The carrier asked if I were C. Endicott, care of the Tillicum Ranch. I said yes, thinking it was a telegram about my business. When I read the message I couldn't believe it!" His face grayed and he looked older than he had since arriving at Tillicum so many months before.

"But I don't understand. How could a business telegram cause you to plan such an ordeal for Cricket?"

"Martha, it wasn't a business telegram." He read aloud, " *'Have ditched Millie. Will be there Tuesday. Dig up local minister or justice of peace or something. We'll go to Hawaii for honeymoon. Signed, Barney Delevan.'* " He lifted up tormented eyes. "Don't you see? I couldn't have her here when he came! She must have been corresponding with this creature or why would he send such a telegram? I knew if I got her up there with Loring she would be safe."

"Safe! You sent your granddaughter off in the company of a young man, knowing they would be trapped in a snowy mountain cabin at least for a few days, and you call it safe? Do you know what can happen up there, how the trees crash down in the snow? Do you know that sometimes it is almost impossible to get the pump thawed and you have to thaw ice and melt snow to get water? Do you have any idea what you have sent her to?"

Fire met fire as the gray eyes met the blue, but Charles only said, "I would trust Loring anywhere on earth to take care of Cricket."

The Ameses couldn't help but be impressed with his sincerity. It took away some of the anger at what this conniving old man had done.

"As soon as I could think over the telegram I asked Loring to take me for a ride. He didn't want to go, but I insisted. That's the day we went to the cabin and got home long after dark. I knew all I had to do was get Cricket set on going and he'd have to take her. Don't you see, it's a matter of life or death! Cricket has changed since she's been out here, she's more of a real person. But if Delevan comes with his dapper New York airs, who is to say that change will be permanent? If she could only have a little more time . . ."

Martha spoke, glancing at the calendar. "But today's Thursday, shouldn't Delevan have been here?" Charles pointed outside.

"Oh yes, he couldn't have made it through the storm," Martha admitted. "The road from Jackson is closed. But just what are you going to tell him when he does get here?" She fixed her gaze sternly on Charles Endicott. He felt the way he had as a small boy when his mother discovered him stealing cookies out of the big kitchen jar.

"I'm going to tell him . . . tell him . . . oh, I don't know! I'll think of something!"

Charles was impatient.

"Have you considered just what your little scheme could do to Loring and Cricket?" The old man grinned then cackled outright.

"For one thing, she will use some of those cooking skills you have taught her. She will also learn to appreciate the value of a roof over her head against the storm, the warmth of a fire, and so on."

"You don't have a very high opinion of Cricket, do you?" Bill's voice held a tinge of contempt, the first Charles had ever known from him. It brought a flush to his face.

"She is what I have made her. Heaven help her for that."

"Well, I think your little joke has gone far enough. When were they to come back?"

"Whenever Loring thought the going was good enough. I thought it might have been today but it's so late now I imagine they will be in tomorrow."

"What if she finds out it was a plan?"

"How could she?" His surprise was genuine. "I'm certainly not going to tell her and neither will Loring. After all, she is the one who insisted on going, she will just remember that. Maybe she will even be sorry she got him into such a mess."

"You really are a schemer." There was no sign of approval in his host's voice. "But, as you say, they should be in tomorrow. What's done is done, but I think in all fairness to Cricket you should tell her the whole story."

"And have her run off and marry Delevan in a fit of anger?" Charles couldn't believe his ears. "Tell Cricket? Never!"

The next day came and went with no Loring and Cricket. By late afternoon even Bill and Martha were beginning to worry. Surely the two would have come out of the mountains today! The weather was better, the going would be hard but not impossible. Why hadn't they come? There were clouds gathering for another downpour. Was there some reason they hadn't come?

It was just before dusk that the knock on the front door echoed weirdly through the big house. The ranch had been isolated since the storm and now the sound of it was strange to their ears. Martha stopped what she was doing, a feeling of premonition and dread going through her. Charles listened intently but Big Bill's deep voice was indistinct from the other room. When he came back to the kitchen his face was pale.

"What is it?"

"That was Sam Sloan." He paused to swallow hard.

"Our nearest neighbor, about a mile

away," Martha supplied for Charles's benefit.

"He has Bay in his barn. He hasn't been able to come, of course, said he thought the horse probably just wandered away from the others. He wanted to let us know he put him up, rubbed him down."

"*Bay!* Loring rode him when they went to the cabin!"

"I know. And Bay came to Sam's *last Monday!*" Martha dropped into a nearby chair. "Then . . ."

"Then Loring and Cricket are in the cabin with one horse between them and another blizzard shaping up!" They had completely forgotten Charles in their new concern but now his words caught them.

"God forgive me, what have I done?" His face blanched and tears tumbled down his aged cheeks. It was agony to see him, to know how responsible he felt. Quickly Martha encircled the thin stooped shoulders with her strong arms.

"Don't worry. They will just have to stay there until we can send help. They'll be all right. Remember, you said you'd trust Cricket with Loring anywhere." Gradually she cheered him up until he ceased shaking. Martha was afraid if he continued he would bring on another heart attack. She remembered Cricket telling how he had almost died before. So with a false sense of cheerfulness she went on, telling him of other times, of times when she and Big Bill and small Loring had been kept inside the cabin. Of the cozy feeling, the big fires. At last she succeeded in getting him to lie down on the couch, but there was no joy in her own face or in her husband's as the old man who had engineered the whole thing finally slipped into a troubled, uneasy sleep.

Several hundred miles away sullen Barney Delevan was still raging at the elements that kept him from his desired goal. He thought he would go mad staying inside, looking out at that hated snow, trying again and again to get through by telephone. At last he had had enough. Another storm was predicted and there seemed no way of going on to Cricket. There was one reservation left for the afternoon train back to New York — if he left immediately before the other storm came.

His decision was made. Not even Cricket was worth all this! He contented himself with sending another telegram, not knowing what havoc he had wrought with the first. The operator told him she didn't know when it would get through but there was nothing he could do about that either.

Cricket would get it sometime. Besides, she was probably as sick as he of this Godforsaken country. She'd be glad enough to get back to little old New York! The thought, along with a couple more drinks, cheered him up as he dictated the telegram.

Sorry, snow held me up. Come to NYC as soon as you can. Better place to get married anyway! Yours, Barney. With a grunt of satisfaction he boarded the eastbound train and made the trip profitable by getting up a card game.

But Cricket neither knew nor cared for Barney Delevan and his troubles. She was facing a fight for life. Evidently some kind of infection or virus had settled on Loring. She wasn't alert enough to diagnose the trouble, she only knew she had a battle on her hands. Loring tossed and turned, alternately hot and cold. She slept little, only catching snatches of naps in the second bunk, always half-awake, constantly piling blankets on him or bathing his face and arms in cold water as his temperature demanded. At times she nearly gave up. She was convinced no one would come now, especially when she looked out the window and saw the signs of another approaching storm. But in the long, dark hours of the night the Cricket who had led society died. In her place, rising triumphantly from the ashes of the dead flame, was a woman who refused to give up. Not while there was breath left in her would she cease doing her best!

The hour came, amid an angry twilight, that Cricket knew was the turning point. Loring had grown weaker; he resisted the broth she had prepared when she tried to force it between his lips. If he didn't get better soon he would die.

What was death anyway? Her tired brain even refused to consider it. If those you loved died, was there any use in living yourself? If only she could believe in eternity, as Loring did.

The thought burned in her brain, bringing her more fully awake than she had been in days. *Loved.* So that was it, she loved Loring Ames. This Wyoming rancher, this guide, this unshaven sick man whose very life depended on the thin thread of her caring . . . *she loved him.*

It was an electric shock, and it vitalized every part of her tired body. Call it a sudden flame; ecstasy; a glow of hope. But even before it was fully born it began to fade. What good to find out now, with him so sick before her? But wait! Why shouldn't the knowledge serve her well? She had heard of people under duress doing unbelievable things; she must do the same.

She looked down at him before her, so helpless and dependent. Tenderness replaced the first quick flash of understanding, and gently she bent low, kissing the lips that had never touched her own. Did she fancy it or was he cooler once more? Did he stir a little in his sleep, almost a slight response? She didn't know. She only knew as she dropped to her knees beside his bed that if he were to die the best part of her would go with him. She had always thought it melodramatic but now she understood.

"You will live," she promised, "you will!" Her cry pierced the layers of unconsciousness that had gradually been lifting. Loring's eyes opened. Glazed with the last traces of pain, filled with wondering where he was, they focused and rested on the tumbled dark head so close to him, bent against the side of the bed. With a mighty effort he lifted one hand and gently placed it on that dark hair. For a moment Cricket couldn't believe it. Then a glorious look crossed her tired, pale face. The man struggled to speak but she placed cool fingers across his lips.

"Later." It was enough. He drifted back off to sleep.

If Cricket had known how to pray she would undoubtedly have shouted thanks to the highest heavens. Yet in spite of her lack of Christian training she felt something inside that was bigger than herself, something above and beyond, that at her lowest moment had brought her to new heights. A Presence that banished despair.

"Thank you," she whispered in the stillness. Quietly she slipped away. When he awoke there must be broth prepared, and this time she was sure he would be able to take it. It was just as she was turning back for a last look at Loring that she spied something unnoticed before. She had been so engrossed with her task of helping him she hadn't looked around the small room where he lay. All her attention had been on the man himself and his tremendous need. Now the turned-down light of the old kerosene lamp she carried caught the glint of a gold frame on the wall. Strange, why hadn't she seen it before? Perhaps because it hung in a dim corner.

As Cricket read the simple words her heart swelled.

"I will lift up mine eyes unto the hills from whence cometh my strength." For the first time she realized the truth, that strength *was* God, Creator of heaven and earth. She bowed her head in surrender. "God, I'm not worth much but I'm yours. Forgive me and

accept me." She hesitated and her lips trembled. What else? Oh, yes — the words Loring had used when he returned thanks the day they arrived at the cabin. "For Jesus' sake, Amen."

Eyes wet, heart uplifted, she rose to her tasks filled with peace unlike anything she'd ever experienced — and the knowledge she could and would, with God's help, take care of Loring until Bill Ames came for his son.

13

Loring's natural strength, combined with Cricket's determination, brought results. He graduated from broth to soft food to "real food," as he called it. Cricket remained aware of his gaze. Any time she stayed inside, his blue look followed her. Sometimes approvingly, at other times puzzled. Did he remember that single kiss? Her face scorched at the thought, and not from the black stove she had finally conquered.

So long as he needed her, she served day and night. When he flatly stated, "I'm the same as well," Cricket let her vigilance slide and slept around the clock.

All that day Loring watched her, collecting a gallery of pictures against the time she would return to his world. He never intended to let her creep into his heart but there she was. Cricket, mounted on the faithful Buckskin. Cricket, incredibly beautiful in his mother's crimson senorita outfit. Cricket, laughing on the stairs with her grandfather over the downfall of Barney Delevan. Cricket, defying him, insisting on coming to the mountains. Cricket, the red stealing under her white skin when he told her they must stay. Cricket, the nurse, the dedicated Cricket who had saved his life.

Never had a man worshiped a woman the way Loring Ames learned to in those days. Although careful to never let it show, his feelings filled him until at times it seemed he must cry out his great love for her. But his lips were sealed. Her great wealth stood between them. Even if she were to turn her back on her native home, the money would still be there. Neither could he become a lap dog, a kept husband, luxuriating in her good fortune. But in spite of the seal he had put on himself, Cricket could feel his love around her. She remembered the night when he had cried out, giving away the carefully concealed plot, admitting he indeed loved her. It warmed her. She wouldn't look ahead, it was enough to have him getting stronger day by day.

And then the day came with brilliance and beauty when they heard crashing outside. It followed several other days of milder weather. Evidently this earlier storm had merely been the preface of what would come later. Even near their cabin the unusual warmth had set eaves dripping.

"It's Dad." Loring's eyes met Cricket's, flickering for a moment. The flash of her dark eyes told him she had discovered the plot.

It was a long hard trip for one who had been sick as Loring, but he gritted his teeth and held on. Cricket suffered with him and wondered if they would have been better off back in the cabin. Yet she was realistic enough to know this false weather could betray them without warning. It was best to get him home on the big wood sledge Bill had brought.

"Doc will be there by the time we are," Big Bill told them and when they finally made it and got Loring inside, the good old doctor checked him from top to toe and then snorted in an undignified way.

"He's fine." The man's voice was gruff; along with everyone else he had known and loved Loring Ames since he was a little tyke. "Thanks to you," he bowed with an old-fashioned courtliness to Cricket, and then he was gone before she could reply. But it was for Martha to take the girl in her arms, exclaiming over her thinness, her eyes that seemed to fill up her whole face. Loring insisted on being carried back downstairs to the couch by the fire. He felt he had to be present when Cricket had it out with her grandfather.

It wasn't long. The minute the doctor and others of the rescue party had gone Cricket marched over to her grandfather.

"Gramps, you've pulled a lot of things in your life. But this tops them all. I've never been so ashamed of you before, never!"

"It was my fault too," Loring had to confess. "How did you know?" She just looked at him.

"You mumbled in your sleep. I figured it out. But why, Gramps?"

Slowly he pulled the worn telegram from his pocket. She read it, tore it to bits, and flung it in the fire.

"Thanks for your high opinion of me." The words were bitter. "You really think I've had anything to do with him since he left? I haven't. I never intended to. Any feeling I might have had was completely drowned out the night Mr. Ames dumped him in the horse trough!" In spite of the gravity of the situation Loring's father simply couldn't help but grin. Cricket caught it and in an instant was joining him in the biggest laugh she had had in months. Loring and Martha chimed in but Gramps only stared into the fire. When he turned to Cricket his chin quivered.

"I'm sorry Cricket, I should have known better. But if you knew what I've gone through since you didn't come back . . ."

"I forgive you, Gramps." In a flash she was at his side. Suddenly all the tears that had been crowded inside during the long, dreadful time in the mountains threatened to overwhelm her.

"But, oh Gramps, Loring could have died!" She suddenly gave way and hot tears poured onto her grandfather's shoulder. Nothing else she could have done would have shown what she had gone through. Cricket wasn't a girl who cried easily; but the dam had burst and there was no stopping the flood.

"Let her cry." It was Loring who understood. "It's a natural reaction. She kept up as long as she had to. Now it's over. She doesn't have to keep up any longer. Let her cry it out." Charles's arms tightened around her. She might have forgiven him, but he couldn't forgive himself, not yet. It was still too new, too fresh. In time perhaps he could hold up his head proudly, but not now. Humility was not one of his traits yet in those moments he was completely humbled.

"Time to get these two off to bed." Martha's brisk tone cleared the air. "I'll bet they'll sleep well tonight!"

Big Bill had the last word. "It's over. Whatever has happened is in the past. There's no use going back over and over it again, placing blame, trying to atone for something that can't be changed. I suggest we pick up living tomorrow as a new day."

His kindly words filled Cricket's thoughts as she prepared for bed. No matter what had happened, regretting or blaming couldn't change it. Then, too, Gramps had done what he thought was for her own good. He couldn't know the horse would run away or that Loring would be hurt. Slipping out of her bed she stole softly into her grandfather's room. She knew he wouldn't be asleep.

"I love you, Gramps," she whispered. He couldn't answer because of the lump in his throat, but the hard squeeze of his hand showed her how much he cared. And this time when she got back to bed, Cricket slept the untroubled sleep of a small child.

Cricket awakened to the smell of cinnamon rolls wafting up from the kitchen. She quickly bathed and slipped into a scarlet wool dress suitable for the cold day. When Loring commented, "You look like a Christmas rose," she blushed until her face matched the dress. But after breakfast she said, "I have an announcement." The apprehensive look on Gramps's face made her rush on. "When things were almost hopeless in the cabin I felt an unknown Presence. I knew it must be your God." Her gaze traveled from Bill to Martha to Loring.

"Then I spied the Bible verse on the wall, the one about strength coming from the hills. I told God that He could have me, even though I wasn't worth much."

The same radiance that had glorified Loring's face a few times before spread until it blinded her. Her heart pounded and the thought came, *Why, I've met his final qualification*. Rich color accompanied the idea and her cheeks felt warm.

Gramps cleared his throat and said humbly, "I did the same, Cricket, after I realized what an ornery old sinner I really was, especially in practically forcing Loring to —"

"We're forgetting that, Gramps," Cricket cut in, but Loring's quick response left her shaken when he quietly disagreed.

"Some of us will never forget the courage and valor that is responsible for me being here right now." A general murmur of assent rose then Bill said, "Let us give thanks."

Cricket had heard him pray many times but the deep note of thanksgiving for their safe return and Charles and Cricket's acceptance of the One Who had died to save them plunged into her heart and glowed in a steady flame.

Not a single eye stayed dry at the end of that prayer. Then Bill grinned. "Well, now the important things are taken care of, it's about time to start planning for Christmas."

November rushed by. Cricket and Charles had taken a thrift pledge and now they chafed under its restrictions. "Couldn't we just bend it a little?" she demanded. "There are so many things I'd like to buy . . ." She shook her head. "No, it would embarrass the Ames family and the hands." She sighed. How much easier to be creative when unlimited funds lay behind her!

"What are you sending Barney Delevan for Christmas?" Gramps teased. Following the Lord hadn't taken the teasing streak out of him.

"The back of me hand, as the Irishman said," she retorted. The overconfident suitor's second telegram lay unanswered in a drawer. Cricket had made up her mind to wait until she could think of something sufficiently final before responding. Now she flared into disgust. "He reminds me of the man who finally said he could take a hint, but only after he'd been kicked down the stairs three times."

Christmas arrived and proved to be all the Ameses had predicted. The Endicotts' new understanding of the true meaning of Christmas added a great deal to their joy. Practical but much appreciated gifts traded hands. Loring's gift to Cricket crowned the holiday. He had taken a section of yellow pine with the bark intact, carved it, and then coated it with layer after layer of varnish. Its words were now familiar:

I will lift up mine eyes unto the hills from whence cometh my help. My help cometh from the Lord, which made heaven and earth.
(Psalm 121:1–2)

At the last minute Gramps gruffly confessed, "I know we agreed to live as you have." He looked at them appealingly. "I hope you won't mind too much that I stretched our agreement. Besides, my gift is a conditional thing, part present, part business." He extended a thick sheaf of papers. "You can read it later but what it boils down to is I'd like to buy into Tillicum Ranch."

Sheer shock descended over the firelit room.

Gramps looked shamefaced but delighted

at his bombshell. "I'd never want a controlling interest. If you'll agree, I thought we could go with 20 percent for each of us — Cricket, myself, and you three. That way I could invest in the ranch and help build up your cattle and horse herds."

"You old dear!" Cricket bounded to him and hugged him hard.

The Ameses still looked dazed but gradually smiles grew.

"It would sure help," Bill admitted, visions of expansion clear in his eyes.

"No more wondering if we'd have to sell when we have a bad year." Martha's comment told more than she intended.

"A partner with you?" Loring took a deep breath. As a partner with Charles Endicott, wouldn't he be far more eligible in case Cricket could ever learn to care for him?

After his magnificent gesture that had appeared so sincere, Gramps tore down everything in one crushing blow. At lunch he announced that as soon as the roads cleared he and Cricket would be leaving for Long Island.

"*What?*" Cricket's voice cracked like a pistol shot.

"You heard me." He raised determined brows. "I do have a business to run and I'm a lot better. It's time we left."

"I'm not going." Cricket lay down her

fork and prepared for battle.

"I beg your pardon?" His silky inflection hid nothing.

"I've had enough of New York — forever. I'm staying here." In an effort to lighten the mood she added, "Now that I own 20 percent of Tillicum Ranch I intend to stay here and protect my investment."

"Haw, haw." Big Bill's mouth stretched wide.

Charles shot him a furious look but merely said, "We're leaving. *Both* of us."

"If the Ameses will let me, I'm staying on." Cricket flung down her napkin and hardened her lips.

Martha nodded. So did Bill, but neither spoke. Loring's muscles tightened like a crouching cougar.

"I say you won't!" Gramps rose and glared at his granddaughter.

Loring shoved back his chair and sprang to his feet in one fluid gesture. His voice stayed low, respectful, yet even his father's smile died at the deadly look he bestowed on Charles. "Sir, since you've turned our lunch into a battlefield, I guess anyone can get in the war. No one — not even you — can talk like that to a woman in our home."

"By what right do you criticize me?" Charles looked at Loring curiously. "Who do you think you are?"

Loring glanced at Cricket, frozen with disbelief, and back at Charles. A poignant light crept into his face. "I'm the man who is going to marry your granddaughter."

"You're *what?*" Gramps sounded choked. "You think Charity Endicott would consider marrying you?"

"No." He actually smiled at his adversary. "But I think that Cricket Lee may." He held out a strong hand to the bewildered girl. "I'm sorry it came like this, dear. I'm a plain Wyoming rancher but I love you second only to my Master — and yours. You have the right to know and choose."

"Cricket," Gramps thundered. "Tell this — this — tell him what you think of him."

She shook her head. Never had she been lovelier. "All right, Gramps." She took Loring's hand. "I'd be proud to marry you and spend the rest of my life here with you."

Gramps's voice sputtered on. "Think of what you're giving up. Money. Position." He hesitated and she swung toward him with velvet-dark eyes ablaze.

"You say I'm like Grandmother. Can you imagine *her* giving up *you* for money or position?"

"Even if I cut you out of my will?" He played his trump card. "Even if I cast you off and no longer consider you my child?"

Cricket's hand tightened convulsively in Loring's. Could she give up Gramps even for Loring? Yet how could she give up Loring, who loved her and had brought her to a knowledge of her Lord, Jesus Christ?

"Even then."

The most beautiful look she had ever seen on her grandfather's face softened the lines. His gray eyes brimmed. "Cricket, Loring, forgive me. I had to know if you love Loring with the kind of love God intended, the only love that can see you through sickness and health, good times and bad."

Loring's fingers gripped hers until she wondered if he'd crush her bones. His sapphire eyes blazed with righteous indignation. "Then this was all some kind of test you dreamed up?"

Gramps didn't budge from the younger man's scorn. "I had the best in marriage. I couldn't bear it if you — either of you — settled for less." A smile lurked in the depths of his eyes. "Besides, I didn't know if you'd ever speak, son, knowing Cricket will inherit millions." A familiar twinkle lighted his face. "Sometimes a little push here and there doesn't hurt."

Loring's face didn't lose its tight expression, even when he told Cricket, "Bundle up and we'll go outside. I need some fresh air."

Hand in hand they silently climbed a nearby hill. The frozen snow easily held their weight and the icy air put red flags in Cricket's cheeks that matched the ones waving in her heart. Loring loved her. He wanted to marry her. A prayer of gratitude wafted upward from a heart too full for words.

"Cricket, I have to ask. Did you really mean it or did anger at your grandfather influence what you said? It's still a hard life."

Somewhere, some time in the past, Cricket had read the expression, "The world held its breath, waiting for an answer." So did the snowy Wyoming landscape. She thought of the cabin episode and her heart quailed at the very thought of how demanding and dangerous this country could be. Could she face another such time, or different but equally perilous events?

The winter sun focused on Loring's dark gold hair as he stood bareheaded before her. Behind him stood the Grand Tetons, their serrated edges slicing the sky. Peace surrounded her. "I will have God and you beside me. Why should I be afraid? I love you, Loring."

With an inarticulate cry he gathered her close. His cold lips sought and found hers and warmed with their kiss. After a long time he released her and gently turned her toward the log lodge with its welcoming, lighted windows. "My darling, let's go home." Together they retraced their footsteps across the frozen pasture and Cricket's heart sang. She had found a hearth and a home where love — and God — would reign.

Epilogue

A few weeks later a simple wedding on Tillicum Ranch united Charity Endicott and Loring Ames in marriage. Over Gramps's protests, only Gramps, Martha and Bill Ames, the ranch hands, and the minister attended.

"Loring would hate the publicity if we did it otherwise," Cricket said and sighed. "This way, David Barrington can write the wedding up while he plans for his own."

Gramps grinned. "Always said Mary, Barney, and David belonged together." He touched her white gown with a gnarled finger. "Cricket, did you ever answer Barney Delevan's telegram?"

"Oh, yes!" She threw back her misty veil and laughed. "This morning."

"Well?" Gramps demanded and a smile twitched his lips.

"The telegram said, *'Due to a previous engagement I won't be meeting you in NYC. Our love to Mary. Signed, Charity Endicott Ames.'*"

The employees of Thorndike Press hope you have enjoyed this Large Print book. All our Large Print titles are designed for easy reading, and all our books are made to last. Other Thorndike Press Large Print books are available at your library, through selected bookstores, or directly from us.

For information about titles, please call:

(800) 223-1244
(800) 223-6121

To share your comments, please write:

Publisher
Thorndike Press
P.O. Box 159
Thorndike, Maine 04986